# A STRANGER AND AFRAID

ELIZABETH FERRARS was born in Rangoon and arrived in England at the age of three. She came to live in East Lothian when her husband was appointed Professor of Botany at Edinburgh University. She comes from an old Scottish family: her maiden name was Mactaggart, and one of her great-grandfathers, Peter Clouston, was Lord Provost of Glasgow.

She was educated at Bedales School, Hampshire, and took a diploma in Journalism at London University, but decided to write novels instead. She has now published more than thirty of them, and many have been translated into Japanese, German and French.

*Available in Fontana by the same author*

Skeleton Staff

ELIZABETH FERRARS

# A Stranger and Afraid

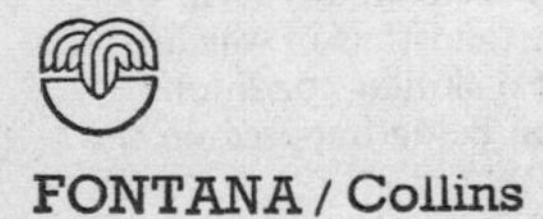

FONTANA / Collins

First published in 1971 by William Collins Sons & Co Ltd
First issued in Fontana Books 1972
Second Impression February 1979



Made and printed in Great Britain by
William Collins Sons & Co Ltd, Glasgow

# CHAPTER I

WHEN A TRAIN arrives late at a London terminus, or at some such place as Manchester or Glasgow, a loudspeaker is liable to offer token apologies from British Railways for the inconvenience caused to everybody, and to tell people that the reason was engine failure, fog on the line, or whatever.

But when a train arrives late at a small station like Helsington, it does so without explanations. The inconvenience suffered by the passengers who alight there may be just as great as at larger stations, but it is not acknowledged.

Not that that makes the slightest difference to anybody.

Humping her large suitcase along the platform after leaving a train that had arrived at five-seven, when it should have done so at four-thirty, and hearing a loudspeaker cackling away overhead, Holly Dunthorne was not offended at hearing no one apologizing to her. She was only intensely thankful that she had no need to make any effort to understand where the voice was telling her to go and what to do. She had been travelling since five o'clock that morning, and loudspeakers, talking at her in a variety of languages, had been baffling her since dawn.

But now she was home. Or at least at one of the places that she was accustomed to thinking of almost as home. She had no more need of instructions. She only had to be prepared, as soon as she was through the barrier, to make a dash for the bus station, in the hope that she might just be in time to catch the five-ten bus for Roydon Saint Agnes.

Without her suitcase, she could have done it easily. She was twenty-two, long-legged, with fair, shining, sun-bleached hair, and was in wonderful health after a fortnight of swimming, sightseeing and gorgeous over-eating in Portugal.

But her suitcase was filled with all the summer clothes that she possessed in the world, together with some warmer things for her return to an English September, some presents from Portugal for a variety of people, and some heavy volumes of Chaucer. For Holly was a student, working for a Ph.D. in English Literature at London University, and even in the vacation had been doing some serious reading.

And to lug that case, Chaucer and all, for two hundred yards in three minutes was too much for her.

She had only reached the entrance to the bus station when the bus for Roydon Saint Agnes swayed haughtily out. She waved at it imploringly, but the driver only looked down at her with that expression of sadistic arrogance on his face which bus-drivers reserve for the people whom they have succeeded in leaving behind, and drove on. She would have to wait two hours for the next bus.

Thumping her suitcase down on the pavement, she swore aloud and as luridly as she knew how. That was not really very luridly. But an elderly man who was passing looked at her in astonishment and disapproval, making it obvious that she confirmed all his worst fears concerning her generation. However, another man, in a Volvo, who could hardly have heard her actual words, but, she supposed, had seen the expression on her face, grinned as he halted the car beside her and asked, 'If it's Roydon you want, have you any use for a lift?'

She said thank you, if that was where he was going, and he got out of the car to open the boot and stow her suitcase away inside it.

Picking it up unwarily, he almost dropped it.

'God, what have you got inside that?' he asked. 'Lumps of coal?'

'No, just things,' she said. 'I'm rather good at packing. You'd be surprised at how much I managed to get in.'

'Not now that I've handled it, I wouldn't.'

He looked about thirty-five and was tall, narrow-shouldered and gaunt, with a bony face and dark eyes under arched black eyebrows. His hair had been black, but it was beginning to turn a rather handsome shade of grey. He was dressed in a light blue sweater and flannel trousers, with a patterned silk scarf at his throat.

When they had got into the car and it had started off after the bus, Holly asked, 'Do you live in Roydon Saint Agnes?'

'No, I'm just dropping in on a friend,' he said. 'Do you? I don't think I've ever seen you there.'

'No,' she said, 'I'm just visiting too.'

'Actually I live in Helsington,' he said.

They had to pause at traffic-lights at the turning into the main street. It was a long, narrow street, with a Woolworth's, a Marks and Spencer's, a Boots, and most of the other landmarks of any English country town, including a splendid, half-timbered and mainly genuine Elizabethan Town Hall, one quite good hotel, the Crown, and a cinema that specialized in astonishingly dirty films.

He went on, 'I'm on my way to visit a friend in Roydon. Lisa Chard. Do you know her?'

'No, I haven't been here for about two years,' Holly said. 'She must be since my time. But I seem to know her name.'

'You should,' he said. 'She's written several very successful plays.'

'Oh, *that* Lisa Chard. Of course I know her. I mean, I know her plays. I've seen two of them, *Designs on Life* and *The Lesser Evil.* They're good aren't they? Horrifically sinister. Is she really living in Roydon? That must be exciting for everybody. Is she at all like her plays?'

'Do you mean, is she horrific and sinister?' He laughed as the car moved forward again. 'I'd say she's a very warm-hearted, down-to-earth person. Perhaps she's just a bit sinister in business matters. I don't think I'd like to get up against her in those.'

'Are you a writer too?' Holly asked. 'Or an actor?'

She thought that that would explain his rather pallid

complexion, his poise and the charm of his voice. It was a very pleasant voice, soft and low-pitched.

But he shook his head.

'I'm an architect. I built a house for Miss Chard in Roydon. That's how I met her. She saw something I'd done and liked it, and when she decided she wanted a country cottage, she got me to do the job. And she likes the result, bless her, which nobody else does. I don't expect you will.'

'Shall we be passing it?'

They had left the main street and were entering the suburbs, that zone of prosperous-looking bungalows built in the 'sixties, most of them with double garages and with picture-windows that give them beautiful views of their neighbours' gardens, that nowadays encircle almost every town.

'It depends where you want to be dropped,' he said. 'But I think I can guess that. Aren't you Judy Dunthorne's niece? I expect you want to be dropped at Cross Cottage.'

'You're absolutely right,' Holly said, 'though I don't know how you knew it.'

'You fit the description.'

'Who's been describing me?'

'Judy herself, of course, at different times. She talks a lot about you. And the Meridens, and various other people. They like to talk about one another in Roydon Saint Agnes. However, basically there's nothing more interesting than gossip, is there?'

Holly did not agree. She thought all kinds of things more interesting than gossip. English Literature, for one, and world peace, and hunger in under-developed countries. For a time too she had thought that the student's rôle in politics was of absorbing interest, but she was getting a little past the age for that. It seemed to be an interest which you automatically grew out of, as you did out of pimples and other problems of adolescence, as you advanced in years. Not that she had suffered from pimples herself, but she had tried very hard to love some male contemporaries who had.

'Whereabouts is Miss Chard's cottage?' she asked.

'She's your aunt's nearest neighbour,' he told her. 'Her house is in a corner of the old orchard that I suppose used to be part of the Meriden farm once.'

'Only it was never the Meriden farm,' Holly said. 'It belonged to Mrs Meriden's family. Their name was Alden. They sold off most of the land to other farmers, when her father got crippled in an accident with some farm machinery. He died a year or two later. And Ben Meriden, of course, was never the least interested in farming. I wonder why they sold the orchard to Miss Chard. They can't need money. They're terribly rich.'

'I expect Miss Chard talked them into it,' he said. 'She saw the spot and wanted it, and what she wants has an odd way of becoming hers.'

Holly gave him a thoughtful look. 'You know, although you talked about her being warm-hearted and so on, you don't really sound as if you like her much.'

'On the contrary,' he said, 'I like her too much. Like everyone else. It's very difficult not to—even if it isn't altogether wise.'

'Why isn't it wise?'

'Just that she's a very self-sufficient person. I don't think I've ever met anyone who needs other people so little. And that can be—hurtful, if you aren't careful. But that doesn't mean she isn't friendly and good-natured. By the way, I haven't introduced myself. I'm Stephen Floyd.'

Holly had realized by then that that was who he was, but she did not want to let him know that she had heard of him before. She had heard of him from Kate Meriden, the daughter of the Meridens whom they had just been talking about, who was Holly's own age and one of her closest friends. Kate had written to Holly recently that an architect, who without any question was one of the most brilliant men in the country, had come to live in Helsington, and that she had fallen in love with him, wholly, desperately and for ever, and that her life was ruined because he wouldn't even notice that she existed, having fallen in love himself with an amoral, middle-aged bitch for whom he had designed a wonderful house in Roydon. And while not taking any of this particularly seriously, knowing the speed and enthusiasm with which Kate could give her heart away, snatch it back and give it away again, Holly was not inclined to betray her confidence to the object of it.

He went on, 'I saw Judy yesterday and she said nothing about your coming. She said you were in Portugal.'

'So I was, but I suddenly thought I'd come back,' Holly said. 'I tried to telephone her when I got to Heathrow, but I didn't get any answer, so I thought I'd just chance it and come.'

'What was the trouble?' he asked. 'The company you were with, or did the money run out? You weren't alone, were you?'

'No, I was with friends. There wasn't any trouble. It was just . . .' She stopped and gave his sharp-edged profile a considering look. 'I haven't been to see Judy for ages,' she added with a certain caution.

'It wasn't that an SOS went out to you from the Meridens about this trouble over Marcus?'

'Marcus?' She was startled. Marcus was Kate's younger brother, just nineteen, and had had next to nothing to do with any action that Holly had ever taken in her life. 'Why, what's happened to Marcus?'

'It's the same sort of thing as last time, only worse,' Stephen Floyd said. 'You know about last time, I suppose.'

'I know he was in court once and fined five pounds for helping to smash up the Sea Cave Dance Hall.'

'Well, he won't get off with a five-pound fine this time, if he's found guilty. This time a man got badly hurt. It's

Grievous Bodily Harm. The case is going to Quarter Sessions.'

'Do you mean Marcus is in gaol?' She felt shock and incredulity.

'Not at the moment,' he said. 'He's out on bail. I think the case is going to be heard in about three weeks' time. His mother's frantic.'

'But he *can't* be guilty, can he? Do you think he is? Has he pleaded guilty?'

'No, in fact he says he wasn't in the place at all at the time, and that's the official family line.'

'Then it's probably the correct one,' Holly said confidently. 'I know Marcus is every kind of fool, but there's absolutely no real violence in him.'

'He pleaded guilty to that other affair, which I understand was pretty violent.'

'But that was just having a drink too many when he wasn't used to it and getting rowdy and punching a policeman. And he did plead guilty without any fuss—isn't that important? I mean, don't you think that's what he'd do now if he'd actually hurt someone?'

Her answer seemed to amuse Stephen Floyd.

'People change as they get older, you know,' he said. 'Sometimes they don't always stay as nice as they were when they were younger.'

'But aren't there witnesses?'

They had left the last houses behind now. On either side of the road there were fields of stubble, divided from one another by hawthorn hedges, red with berries. In one field some pheasants paraded in splendour, the late September sunlight striking glints of flame and copper from their plumage. Ahead were the roofs of Roydon Saint Agnes, showing among trees, with the squat tower of the church in the midst of them.

'He says there was a witness,' Stephen Floyd said, 'but she says there wasn't.'

'She?'

'A girl. Loraine Something. I've forgotten her name. I've heard the story so often during the last couple of weeks that I've stopped listening to it properly. She's an actress at the Market Theatre. D'you know about the Market Theatre? It's a new repertory we've acquired in Helsington. Miss Chard takes a lot of interest in it. Anyway, this Loraine girl says she wasn't with Marcus at all when he says she was—and if you're still interested, there's my house—I should say Miss Chard's house—and I'm quite prepared to be told it's a horror and desecrates the landscape, but I should say too that I myself think it's pretty good. I wish I could afford to live in something like it.'

There was the house, a collection of white cubes, dumped on each other at random, so it seemed at first sight, at a spot where, for as long as Holly could remember, there had never been anything but old apple trees, bowed to the ground with age, standing among brambles and briars. The place had been wonderful for blackberrying, and in the spring for primroses and some specially sweet-scented white violets. A good deal of the wilderness was still there, but the house in the corner of it made an uncompromising statement of human invasion.

'There, I told you you wouldn't like it,' Stephen Floyd said, with a painful sort of triumph in his voice, as if he felt satisfaction at hurting himself before Holly had a chance to do it.

'But I'm not sure I don't like it,' she said as they left the house behind. It was not merely that she was a good-natured girl. She really had not made up her mind what she thought of it. She only knew that she resented it for being there at all. But that was hardly Stephen Floyd's fault. 'It's so new and so surprising, you see. There was never anything there before, and when we were kids, Kate and Marcus and I, we used to play all kinds of games there. There were lots of little tunnels in under the brambles and things, if you knew where to look for them, and we'd go crawling about there, being outlaws and spacemen and so on. Marcus used always to trail after Kate and me, not wanting to be left out, and we'd get so bored with him because he was just a boy and too young for us that we'd be beastly to him. But I was very fond of him really. He was always, he still is, or was when I saw him last . . .' She hesitated, trying to find the right word to describe Marcus Meriden, and the only one that she could think of made her feel self-conscious. But she used it all the same. 'He's an extraordinarily *beautiful* sort of boy, isn't he? I'm not sure if that says what I mean, but there's always been something special and different about him. Don't you think so?'

'It would seem that he thinks so himself,' Stephen Floyd said drily, 'and is working quite hard to prove it. But I'm just a man, I may not see what you do.' He stopped the car outside Judy Dunthorne's cottage. 'But I'll say this for him, I don't think he's ever had a chance, growing up in that family. Not the ghost of a chance. A father who's a genius, granted, but totally irresponsible. A hopelessly permissive but wildly possessive mother. An elder brother who simply clears out to Canada and doesn't help. And a lovely but brainless sister. No, things can't be easy for him.'

'But they're a marvellous family!' Holly exclaimed in astonishment and anger. 'Not just Marcus—all of them. I love them. I always have.'

'I should think, before you're through, you'll love a lot of people who aren't worth it. And why not? Don't we all, at some time of our lives?'

He got out of the car and went round it to open the door for her.

She was so hot with rage at what he had said about her friends that she had temporarily lost the power of speech. Sudden anger often had that effect upon her. She would simply stare straight ahead of her blankly, struck dumb by the violence of her own feelings. What might erupt out of her, once she had got used to the violence, was anybody's guess. She never knew herself what was coming. And in this case Stephen Floyd did not wait to find out. Putting her suitcase down on Judy's doorstep, he got back into the car, drove on to the crossroads that had given Cross Cottage its name, turned the car there and drove back again, on his way, Holly supposed, to Lisa Chard's house. In passing he gave Holly a smile and a small wave. She did not return either.

Cross Cottage was built of grey stone and had a roof of uneven red tiles. There was no front garden, except for a strip of grass about a yard wide, edged by white wooden posts with chains slung between them, and with a big lavender bush at each side of the doorstep. Some of the building was said to date back to the seventeenth century, some to the eighteenth, and some of it, containing such things as a bathroom and an excellent little kitchen, had been added on during the last twenty years. But all the additions had been made in the same kind of stone, and as stone has no easily measurable age, it all blended together, a bit of a jumble, but pleasing, looking as if it had grown where it stood, bit by bit, as the tall beeches that flanked it on both sides had grown, with grey lichen on their bark and thick, black leafmould under them.

Holly stood there in the road, thinking fiercely, 'Not the ghost of a chance! He said Marcus never had a ghost of a chance, growing up in a family like the Meridens!'

What would she not have given herself to have belonged to a family like the Meridens? She was an only child and her home had generally been a flat in London, if her parents had happened to be in England, which a lot of the time they were not, as her father was an engineer who worked for a big oil company and was sent here and there, all over the world, for three or four years at a time. When Holly was a young child, he and her mother had generally taken her with them, but once they had begun to worry about her education she had been left behind at a boarding-school, spending most of the holidays with Judy, her father's sister. And warmly as she had always loved Judy, it had been a devout, private prayer of Holly's that somehow, by some miracle, she might come to belong to the Meriden family, who lived in a lovely big house, went to a wonderful school in Helsington where no one did any work if he didn't want to, because that was much better for his character than living by rules, and who were all, in their different ways, unlike anyone else whom she had ever met.

Mounting Judy's doorstep now, she banged on the door with the wrought-iron knocker.

No one answered the knock, and after a moment Holly tried the door-handle, found that the door, as usual, was unlocked, pushed it open and entered.

There was a small, dark hall inside with heavy beams in the low ceiling, a steep, narrow staircase mounting on the left, with the door to the kitchen under it, the door into the sitting-room on the right and the door into Judy's study facing her.

The study was a small room with a large office desk in it, with a typewriter, a telephone, a lamp and neat piles of typing paper on the desk, a typist's chair, some filing cabinets and a bookcase that covered half a wall. The bookcase contained all the works of Judy Dunthorne in hard covers, paperbacks and translations. They were children's books and writing them brought Judy a comfortable income to supplement what she had inherited from her parents, which had not been much. Also, the work was an outlet for her formidable energy. She had so much that Holly, thirty years younger than Judy, sometimes found it exhausting to keep up with her.

Judy was not in the study now. She worked in the mornings, regularly and punctually, from nine-thirty to twelve-thirty, while Mrs Gargrave, who had worked for her for eleven years, cleaned the house. Then Judy would put the cover on the typewriter, straighten all the papers on her desk, help herself to one glass of sherry, which she would drink on the terrace at the back of the house if it was warm enough, and in the sitting-room if it was cold or wet, and so gradually relax into an easy-going and accessible person. A person who presently, when she felt like it, would make herself a sandwich and a cup of coffee and would have plenty of time, for the rest of the day, for village activities, of which she was always in the thick, and for taking an interest in her garden and her neighbours.

Holly had heard it said, too much of an interest. But she thought that this was simply that Judy lived in a very small world and felt that everything that happened in it was immensely important.

Holly's guess now was that she would find her in the garden. On an afternoon such as this, which felt a little chilly after Portugal, but which was sunny, windless and full of a fragrance that only just hinted at the autumn, it was most unlikely that Judy would be in the house. All the same, before going any farther, Holly stood still in the hall and called out, 'Hallo—it's me!'

When there was still no answer, she put her suitcase down and went to the door of the sitting-room.

It was in the eighteenth-century part of the house, and was much higher and lighter than the hall and the study. It was furnished with some comfortable armchairs in faded covers, a few, small, pretty Early Victorian tables and stools, some bookshelves that bulged untidily with paperbacks and magazines, jammed in along with leatherbound classics, and a good deal of clutter, in the way of Staffordshire teapots, lustre mugs, Bohemian glass and photographs.

The room reached from the front to the back of the house. It had a window that overlooked the road, and a french window that overlooked the small paved terrace at the back, from which a few steps led up to a lawn, which sloped up gently to the encircling woods. The glass door was open now and through it Holly saw Judy on a step-ladder, picking apples.

Holly strolled out on to the terrace and again called out, 'Hallo!'

Startled, Judy clung to a branch of the apple tree, looked round over her shoulder, and exclaimed, 'Holly—I thought you were in Portugal!'

'I was, but I thought I'd come back,' Holly answered.

'Why?'

Holly had not worked out the right answer to this question. She had had a very special reason for coming home, of course, but she did not want to talk about it just yet.

'I just suddenly thought I'd come,' she said, as she had to Stephen Floyd. 'Is it all right? I did try to telephone from Heathrow about one o'clock to ask how you'd feel about it, but nobody answered.'

Judy had scrambled down from the ladder and came towards her. She kissed Holly warmly.

'It's very much all right. I must have been out having lunch with Isobel in Helsington when you phoned. She wanted to talk over this business of Marcus. He's in trouble with the police again, isn't it sickening? What's gone wrong with the boy? He's really such a dear. So Isobel and I went to the Crown. I haven't been there for ages. It's been given a face-lift lately. The food's become quite tolerable, though it's got dreadfully expensive. I'd have enjoyed it if Isobel hadn't been so worried. But now I'm sorry I went, because if I'd known you were coming I'd have met you with the car. How did you get here? You're too early for the bus.'

Judy was a short, muscular woman, with grey hair which she wore cropped very short in a mat of stiff curls, deeply weathered skin, a wide, good-humoured mouth, good teeth and light blue, innocent eyes. Their innocence was real, uncompromising and disconcerting. She could never see evil in anyone. She was wearing scarlet jeans, a darker red jersey and rope-soled sandals.

With an arm round Holly's shoulders, she drew her back into the sitting-room.

'There goes the bus now,' Judy said as it passed the window that faced the road. 'How *did* you get here?'

'I missed the bus and was given a lift by a man who said his name was Stephen Floyd,' Holly answered.

'That was lucky—though you know quite well you shouldn't accept lifts from strange men. I hope you don't often do it. But of course Stephen's harmless.' Judy pulled off her gardening gloves. 'I'd better wash my hands.'

She led the way to the kitchen, a very attractive little place, done in pale yellow and grey, with all the gadgets a woman by herself could want.

Washing her hands under the tap, she went on, 'I suppose Stephen was going to visit Lisa Chard. The dramatist. Did you know we've got her living in the village? She's a very nice woman, not at all spoilt by her success and very kind and helpful. When I had 'flu badly in the spring, she kept trotting in with bottles of wonderful brandy and pot-plants and things. I haven't felt so cherished for years.'

'I should think it's nice for you, having another writer living so close,' Holly said.

'Oh goodness, we never talk about writing,' Judy said. 'I don't exist for her as a writer. Does anyone make films of my books or even use them on television? But I give her advice about her garden and the oddities of village life, and she seems to enjoy that. Now we'll have tea, shall we? I think it's warm enough still to have it out of doors. And while I'm getting it, you could be making your bed—you know where the sheets and everything are, and of course it's the same room as always—and if it's a bit dusty, please don't take any notice of it, because Mrs Gargrave and I have a bit of a thing on at the moment. Fantastic after eleven years, isn't it, but there it is. We're barely on speaking terms. So she's pretending her varicose veins are bad, because she doesn't really want to lose the job, and I'm just letting the house get dirty, because I hope she'll be back soon. Of course, I'd have cleaned things up if I'd known you were coming. Darling, I'm so delighted you *have* come. It's been too long since you did, and all those lunches in London aren't the same. Somehow one never has time to talk about all the things one wants to. And I've lots and lots to tell you.'

Judy always talked a great deal when she had the chance, because in spite of having plenty of friends, she was basically a rather lonely woman. While her parents were alive, she had given all her energy to looking after them, and when they died, one soon after the other, she had been left high and dry.

Now she gave Holly an affectionate slap on her bottom which directed her towards the stairs, then turned to the sink to fill the kettle for tea.

Holly took her suitcase up to the spare bedroom.

It was in the oldest part of the house, with a very low ceiling and a jigsaw puzzle of oak beams in its white walls. The one in which the small leaded window was embedded was about a yard thick. The window was framed in pink and white spotted muslin curtains and overlooked the road. Holly went to the window, opened it and stood there for a moment, leaning on the sill.

From there she could see the white house where Lisa Chard lived. Perhaps, she thought, it would seem all right when you got used to it. As a matter of fact, she was beginning to see a certain charm in it already. It looked cool and clean. But that did not make her any more inclined to forgive Stephen Floyd for the things that he had said about the Meridens. There was a rich fund of loyalty in Holly, and when she thought of his attack upon them, she began to feel rage surging up inside her again.

Ten minutes later, having made the bed, taken a sweater out of her bag and put it on over her cotton dress, gone downstairs and emerged on the terrace, where Judy was just putting a tea-tray down on the green-painted iron table, Holly asked, 'This trouble of Marcus's, Judy—is it really as serious as it sounds? Your Mr Floyd told me something about it.'

Judy poured out the tea. 'I'm afraid it is pretty bad. Isobel thinks it is. She talked about it for two solid hours over lunch. But if you want to know about it, why don't you go over to the Meridens when you've had tea and get it all from the horse's mouth? Don't you remember, that's the first thing you used always to do when you got here to stay with me from school? You couldn't wait to rush over and see Kate. I used to feel mortally offended that you didn't simply want to stay here alone with me.'

'Wouldn't you feel mortally offended if I did that now?' Holly asked, trying not to sound too eager as she took a buttered scone from the plate that Judy pushed towards her.

'My dear, I've got to consider what we're going to eat this evening,' Judy said. 'I was going to have a chop, but you can't split a chop in two, so it'll have to be eggs, I expect. And I might make an apple tart—the apples are fabulous this year. And I've been working all the afternoon in the garden, so I'd like a bath. So if you want to go over, I should, only don't be too long, because we could have a drink together before dinner, and some time this evening Stephen's coming in to look round and advise me on whether I could build a room out over the garage, with a door straight into it from my bedroom, so that I could work up there really by myself and never be interrupted by Mrs Gargrave. It would be very convenient if it could be done, only of course I don't want to spoil the look of the house outside. And if you were here when Stephen comes, you could tell me what you think. I know he's very clever, but I'd like your advice too.'

'What's this thing you mentioned about Mrs Gargrave?' Holly asked.

'Well, it's really all mixed up with Marcus,' Judy said. 'It's very depressing. I suspect I may have stuck my oar in where it may have done more harm than good. Sometimes, the more you try to help people, the less they like it. Anyway, what happened—what's supposed to have happened—is that a group of boys set on one of the porters, quite an old man, at the Sea Cave and beat him up. Isn't it horrible? He has some internal injury, three cracked ribs, cuts on his face that had to be stitched up, and a broken wrist. And Marcus was one of the boys. So several people say. They say they saw him there, kicking the man when he was on the floor. Marcus himself says he wasn't there at all at the time. He says he'd been there earlier, but left before the trouble started. He says he went there with Loraine Gargrave, but he didn't like the way things were shaping up that evening, because there were some of the boys there who only go to the place when they want to make trouble, so when they began to play up, he and Loraine left and went for a drive. And that would be fine if Loraine agreed with him, but both she and Mrs Gargrave say she was at home the whole evening.'

'Loraine Gargrave?' Holly said. 'Mrs Gargrave's granddaughter? That shrimp of a child she sometimes brought with her when she came to work here and used to park in the kitchen, where she ate up all your chocolate biscuits?'

'That shrimp of a child,' Judy said, 'is a very beautiful seventeen now. She lives with Mrs Gargrave still because her mother ran off with someone and her father married again and went to live in Liverpool, and the new wife wasn't keen on being burdened with Loraine, while Mrs Gargrave, of course, was mad to keep her. And it turns out she's got a certain amount of talent as an actress, and Lisa Chard helped to get her taken on at the Market Theatre, and she's said to be very promising. And Marcus is working with them too, scene-painting or something. I don't know if he's any good, but you know no one's ever been able to resist him if he wants something, and he says scene-painting is the dream of his life. So Isobel pretends to be delighted, though she isn't really. She was awfully disappointed when he refused to go to a university. She won't admit it, but she was. But she didn't oppose him when he said what he wanted to do—that would be against her principles—and at least he's stuck to the work for nearly a year, which I think is longer than Kate's ever stuck to anything. So things didn't look too bad till this miserable thing happened.'

'And what's the truth?' Holly asked. 'What Marcus says or what the Gargraves say?'

Judy helped herself to a scone. 'I find it so hard to make up my mind about people,' she said. 'I've always taken for granted that Mrs Gargrave was the soul of honesty. And I've never doubted that Marcus was honest either, though he's got a rather lively imagination. But now we've got two flat statements that contradict each other. And I don't see how anyone can know for certain which is true except the people concerned. And Mrs Gargrave is absolutely determined that Loraine shan't go into court and perhaps get some bad publicity now that she's just started on her wonderful new career, and I was so shocked at her attitude I let her see it, and she went straight off and had trouble with her veins. Which is sickening, because, apart from anything else, I do hate housework, and I'll really have to do some soon if she doesn't come back.'

'I'll help,' Holly said. 'You can set me to work tomorrow. But can't Loraine be subpoenaed or something?'

'What's the good of that if she's made up her mind not to tell the truth and her grandmother backs her up? And perhaps what they say really is the truth. There's that to consider. Now why don't you run over to the Meridens while I have my bath? You might be able to cheer them up a little. They need it. By the way, Andrew's home from Canada—did you know that? Poor Andrew, coming home for just a few weeks after four years and walking smack into this affair. Do go over. But don't be late back, because I'd really like you to be here when Stephen comes.'

She picked up the tea-tray and went indoors with it.

Standing up too, Holly yawned and stretched, just as if she were really not in any hurry, then set off up the garden towards the Meridens' house.

## CHAPTER II

'HOLLY!'

The voice of Marcus's father, Ben Meriden, came from the doorway of the thatched stone barn behind the house. Holly had come to it by the short cut through the beechwood and across the bracken-covered slope beyond it, with the sinking sun in her eyes most of the way. Ben was standing there in flannels and a curious garment that he was fond of wearing, which had pockets everywhere, in which he carried pencils, rulers, screw-drivers and other small tools. He had had that jacket, or others just like it, for as long as Holly had known him. When she thought of him, it was always dressed just as he was now. It suited him. In anything else he looked a little grotesque. He was very wide in the shoulders, with unusually long arms, a muscular, big-boned body and shorter than average legs. Holly had heard him assert that the original idea concerning him in the mind of his Maker had been that he should be a chimpanzee, but that in a moment of abstraction, some humanity had been allowed to slip in. The most purely human thing about him were his hands. They were broad and hard like the rest of him, but delicate and precise in every movement.

He did not come forward to meet Holly but stood waiting for her to go to him in the doorway of the barn. That was like him. He generally expected people to come to him, and did not go out of his way to meet them.

The barn contained his workshop. Once, long ago, before he had married Isobel Alden, he had actually lived in it. He had slept in a camp bed in one corner, washed at a tap in the yard, and done his cooking on a Primus. The rent he had paid the Aldens had been something like fifteen shillings a week. Isobel's father had recently had the accident in which he had lost a leg, and had decided to give up trying to farm his land, and Isobel had persuaded him to let a penniless young genius, whom her friend, Judy Dunthorne, had discovered, have the unused barn for a song. Not that it had been a song for Ben, with nothing but a very small inheritance to get started on, making the beautiful furniture which no one could afford to buy. And even to this day, when his name was known internationally among people who cared for such things, the furniture which he designed and made with his own hands was, economically speaking, just a costly failure.

'I thought you were in Portugal,' he said as he wrapped his long arms round Holly and kissed her.

'I was, but I've just come back,' she said.

'Good.' He was not a man to ask for explanations. She could have told him that she was leaving for Greenland next day without his being really curious to know why. The actions of other people never signified much to him unless they impinged on his own. Then he could be fiercely interested and occasionally ruthless.

He went on, 'You're looking very well and very pretty. Come inside and tell me what you think of a pretty thing I'm making. It's been commissioned by a newcomer to the village, Lisa Chard. I expect you've heard of her. A woman with both taste and money. What a wonderful combination that is, Holly! When you grow older you must arrange to have it. With your natural advantages, you'll find it'll come with trying. If you want it, you know. Particularly the money. That's the important thing, to want it enough. Now come and tell me what you think of it. It's a coffee table—sycamore inlaid with bog oak. I'm having a wonderful time with it. I haven't enjoyed myself so much for ages.'

He did not look as if he were enjoying himself, or were having a wonderful time with anything. He looked unusually tired and worried. But with an arm round Holly's shoulders, he drew her into the workshop.

It was a place she loved. There was a delightful scent everywhere, delightful, at any rate, to her, though perhaps some people would not have cared for that mellow mixture of wood shavings and glue. The walls of the long, lofty place were painted white. The bench stood at one end. It was about seven feet long with a great heavy top with a vice at each end of it, holes in it for bench-pegs and a bench-well at the back, filled with planes and odd fragments of wood. Above the bench was a rack, holding chisels and screw-drivers, and on the wall above that a row of pegs from which hung saws and quantities of sash cramps.

Against another wall was a brassbound tool chest. There was a lathe too, of course, the nearest Ben came to a compromise with mechanization. Under it was a rack containing long-handled chisels and gouges for turning. And there were piles of different kinds of wood, pear and cherry and yew tree and sycamore. Ben only worked in home-grown timbers.

The coffee table that Ben had been making for Lisa Chard was nearly finished. It was long, low, narrow and, as all his work was, supremely elegant. There was never any heaviness or coarseness about it. The bog oak inlay, complex and delicate, showed up as dark as ebony against the pale sycamore.

'It's gorgeous,' Holly said with awe. 'How much will it set her back?'

'Between friends, only about two hundred pounds, I think,' he answered, grinning. He had an off-hand way of talking about his work, rarely sounding as if he took it entirely seriously. Yet you could not have made a bigger mistake than letting that fool you. He took it more seriously than anything else in his life, including his wife and his three children. That was a fact which they all recognized and accepted and of which, Holly had sometimes thought, they were really intensely proud. Their family life revolved around Ben's dedication.

'It must be nice to be rich,' she said.

'Get married and I'll make you something just as pleasant as a wedding-present,' he promised.

She laughed. 'Oh, but we'd have to ditch everything else we possessed, shouldn't we, because the poor things would all be so shamed by the splendid stranger? We'd just have to sit around it on cushions and pretend to be Japanese. Ben, about Marcus . . .'

'Oh, you've heard about that already, have you?' There was irritation in his voice. 'I thought, since you'd only just got here, we might manage to talk about something else. Marcus and his idiocy have been the only subject we've been allowed to talk about for the last fortnight. What a fool the boy is, taking up with the crowd he's got in with! I'm bored with it. Isobel's desperate, of course. The worry and the shame of it, you know, just as if it were all her fault and the boy hadn't got a character of his own. Which perhaps he hasn't, I don't know. She's always telling me I don't know my own children. But it's a bit late to worry about it now. He's practically grown-up and he is what he is for better or worse. Don't you agree?'

Holly found this a rather intimidating attitude. But there had always been something intimidating about Ben, even when he was in a good temper, which was by no means always. Like Marcus, he was capable of explosions of wrath which rocked the household.

'I don't know,' she said warily.

Ben bared his fine teeth in a sardonic grin. 'You don't agree. You think I'm callous. Isobel thinks I'm callous. She thinks I ought to be in sackcloth and ashes, and incidentally proclaiming my belief in the boy's guilt, of which I'm not nearly as convinced as she is, although I know he's a liar and it's stupid to believe a word he says. Isobel always believes the worst of people, have you noticed that? Then she makes up excuses for them, to show how understanding she is, and goes blundering in to help them escape the consequences of their own actions. I prefer to let them get on with their lives with as little interference from me as possible.'

It might have sounded callous to Holly if she had not known that Ben always understated his own feelings, and if she had not already noticed the undertone of pain in his voice. She believed that a lot of his irritation now came simply from frustration at not being able to help Marcus more than he could.

'On the whole, then, you do believe Marcus was with Loraine Gargrave when he said he was,' she said.

'Oh, you know all the details already, do you?' he said. 'You haven't lost much time. I suppose you heard it all from Judy. What a talker that woman is.' His heavy brow twitched in a momentary scowl, almost as if he hated Judy for talking, and his voice grated with an unfamiliar harshness. He was a good deal more on edge, Holly thought, than he wanted her to realize.

'Will Marcus go to gaol if he's convicted,' she asked, 'or will it be just a fine?'

'If it's a fine, he can damned well pay it himself!'

Then Ben laughed and laid one of his great hands on her shoulder. 'But run along in, Holly dear, and talk to the others, if you really want to know it all. I've had all I can take, and I'd like to go on tinkering here for a bit. It's a soothing occupation. Are you staying to dinner?'

'No, Judy wants me specially to go back,' she answered.

'Pity, but I'll be in presently anyway, and perhaps you'll still be there. I expect you'll find Kate at home. Andrew too. Did you know he's home from Canada? Isobel's out, I think. I saw her go to the garage and take the car out a little while ago. And God knows what Marcus is doing. I don't suppose he knows himself.'

His arm propelled her gently towards the doorway, dismissing her.

Crossing what had once been the farmyard behind the house and which now was a paved courtyard with the double garage as well as the workshop opening off it, Holly went round the house to the front door. The twilight was deepening and the chill in the evening was stronger. There was a feeling of moisture in it too, as if it might be going to rain. She wished that she had put on something warmer than the knitted sweater that had seemed enough at tea-time. She rang the bell.

Kate, who answered it, raised her eyebrows in faint surprise at seeing her, remarked inevitably that she had thought Holly was in Portugal, and said nothing about being glad to see her. But Kate never did. She always picked up the threads of their old friendship just as if Holly had never been away, so what would the point have been of saying anything about being specially glad to see her? No one would have expected it of her if the two of them had seen each other yesterday.

Kate led the way to the drawing-room.

She was several inches taller than Holly, and very slender, with a long, slim neck on which a small head was beautifully poised. It was crowned with a mass of smooth brown hair. Everything about her, her eyebrows, her small mouth, her hands, her narrow feet, was delicately shaped. Only a slight lack of animation, which Holly had sometimes thought she was simply too lazy to produce, prevented her from being a real beauty. She could look so vacant, so inattentive, that she appeared stupid, which she was not. She had a shrewd and quick ironic mind, when she troubled to use it. But she spent so much of her time in a hazy dream-world that a number of people who did not know her as well as Holly did were quite unaware of her intelligence.

Kate was dressed now in a pale blue corduroy trouser suit and wore long, glittering ear-rings. Drifting ahead of Holly into the drawing-room with casual, loping strides, she switched on lights, then went straight to a tray of drinks on a table under a big Florentine mirror. The table and most of the furniture in the room, except for the big, comfortable chairs, had been made by Ben. It was of English walnut, moderately solid, but still very graceful, and like everything else that he had made, possessed a distinction of its own. The room was long and high, with a curved bay at one end, pierced by three tall windows which overlooked a somewhat tangled garden, which was gradually disappearing now into twilight. Like Cross Cottage, the house had been added to at so many times that it was impossible to say to what period it belonged, but this room was definitely Georgian, with a marble fireplace and a plaster cornice of looped garlands.

'Well, at least now you've come, I can have a drink,' Kate observed. 'What'll you have? Gin-and-something? The sherry's foul. Mother has one of her attacks of economy on, and we're experimenting with one low form of the stuff after another. Naturally it works out very expensive, as so many of her ideas do, because we all stick to gin or whisky.'

Holly answered that sherry would suit her all the same, and Kate poured it out and handed it to her. Then, sloshing rather a lot of gin into a glass and adding only a dash of tonic, Kate draped herself on the arm of a chair and at once began talking about herself.

'Isn't it absurd, Holly,' she said, 'just now when you came I was desperate for a drink, but I've got fearful inhibitions about drinking by myself. I'm afraid, if I start it, I'll turn into an alcoholic or something. Actually I've got an awful lot of inhibitions, just as if I'd grown up under a rod of iron, instead of generally being allowed to do just as I like. And d'you know, somehow that feeling of being able to do just what I want to is helping me to get desperate about everything? Don't you ever get desperate? I know you don't look as if you do, but don't you ever?'

'Of course I do,' Holly said.

Kate shook her head slightly, as if she did not want Holly's desperation to compete with hers.

'Sometimes I feel it a bit more, sometimes a bit less,' she said. 'But I mean to say, Holly, I'm not getting anywhere, am I? Look at you, you've a degree, you've started working for another, soon you'll become a scholar, or perhaps a journalist, or you'll get a job with the BBC or something, and you'll probably turn into someone fearfully important. And look at me, not even married. Even getting married seems to take something I haven't got. I don't know what. Sometimes I've worked at it quite hard, but there seems to be something about me that stops men dead in their tracks. I've been told I'm too obvious. Then again, I've been told I don't take enough genuine interest in other people. Do you think that's true?'

Holly had sat down and sipped some of the sherry, which was almost as bad as Kate had said it was, and wondered how long this particular experiment in economy on Isobel's part would last. She was always experimenting in economy. Holly had never been in any household where there were so many discussions of the possible edible properties of the cheaper cuts of meat, where the mileage per gallon of different makes of car was so often argued about, and the problem thrashed out of the precise moment at which it would be most profitable to trade in one of the old cars for a new one. Isobel, who had been rich all her life, seemed to have a compulsion to play at poverty. She would not have the resident domestic help that she could easily have afforded, but had the house cleaned by two women who came in from the village, while she herself did the cooking. And as it happened, since she was a superb cook, Holly thought that her family would not have been at all pleased if she had brought someone else in to do the job for her. But suddenly Isobel would be gripped by horror at the expensiveness of some ingredient that she was in the habit of using, and would then avoid it for a week, or a whole fortnight, while her family mocked her for it, argued, and finally, if she tried out something too destructive of their comfort, grew cantankerous. But they had never managed to cure her.

'I don't think you take *any* interest in other people,' Holly told Kate. 'Speaking for myself, it's one of the things I've always liked about you. You're one of the very few people I've ever met with whom one simply doesn't have to pretend at all, because you wouldn't notice it if one did. And I don't see why it should stop you getting married. Lots of married people don't take any interest in each other. By the way, I was given a lift from Helsington by Stephen Floyd. I hope you aren't fearfully interested in him still, because I didn't take to him much.'

Kate looked weary. 'Now there I tried, Holly, I honestly did. I thought I might manage to go really overboard for that cadaverous sort of charm of his. And for a little while I did. I really thought I knew what that sort of thing was all about. But it just wore off. Luckily for me, because he's got other preoccupations. You know, truly, if I knew how to get really interested in anything, I would. I'd work at it like mad, whether it was art, or a job, or politics, or marriage and childbearing—anything, I tell you, just as Ben and Isobel have their full-time occupations in life, Ben his furniture and Isobel the family. And Andrew's never wanted to be anything but a mathematician from the time he was ten, and now Marcus has this theatre thing in his blood, or anyway, Lisa Chard says he has, and got him in with the Market Theatre crowd. You haven't met her, have you?'

Holly shook her head, drinking down some of the syrupy fluid in her glass.

'What's she like?'

'She's a force of destruction.'

'Cripes!'

'Oh, I mean it,' Kate said. 'There *are* people like that, you know. They may be the nicest people in the world, who don't mean an atom of harm to anyone, yet they spread disaster all around them. I think Lisa's like that. She's nice, but she's desperately dangerous. One thing after another has gone wrong since she came to live here, and nearly always when she was trying hardest to be specially helpful. And I feel it in my bones that we haven't got to the end of things yet.'

'Are you blaming her for what's happened to Marcus?'

'Yes, I am. I told you, it's her doing he's got in with the crowd he goes with these days.'

'Are they so awful at the theatre, then?'

'Oh no, it isn't the theatre people who are the trouble. Some of them are marvellous. It's the hangers-on. He's just a hanger-on himself, of course, in spite of what he says. It won't last with him, any more than that kennel-maid business lasted with me. It's one thing to be fond of dogs, I found, and quite another to look after them for eight hours every blessed day. What d'you think, Holly, I've just got registered at the Domestic Science School in Helsington. I don't know why I did it, except that I got so bored trying to be a landscape gardener after being a kennel-maid that I utterly refused to go back to that awful place where they were supposed to be teaching me. And Isobel seemed to think I'd be letting her down if I didn't shine at something. Then Lisa said Domestic Science schools were the end and that if you really want to learn to cook in the great tradition, which I never said I did, the thing was to get apprenticed in a good restaurant, and sweat away in the steam, making sauces under the eye of a good chef, or else just settle down with a shelf of cookery books and work it out for yourself. So I thought to hell with all that, and signed on at the school.'

'Just to spite her?'

'Not exactly,' Kate said. 'I told you, she's nice really.

But just to show I won't grovel under her feet, like everybody else.'

'Why don't you at least go to a school somewhere else?' Holly asked. 'London, for instance. You could share my flat.'

She had an idea that a change would be good for Kate, who had never been away from home for more than a few weeks at a time. She had never been to a boarding-school. Like her brothers, she had been sent to the very progressive day-school in Helsington, where the habit of concentrated work had never been thought of as an important part of character formation. Of course, if you wanted to work, they didn't actually stop you, and Andrew had emerged from the place an unusually able mathematician, and after Cambridge had gone off to a good job with a computer firm in Canada. But if you preferred to spend most of your time slapping paint about, or to express yourself in amateur theatricals, or just to go and climb trees, they didn't stop that either.

'Thanks,' Kate said. 'But face it, if it's cooking I'm going to dedicate myself to, from shepherd's pie to *haute cuisine*, I could hardly find a better teacher than Isobel, could I? So why go away at all, even to that awful place in Helsington? I couldn't be half as comfortable anywhere else as I am at home. Honestly, isn't Isobel the most fabulous cook you ever came across?'

From the hall a voice called out, 'Is that someone saying something nice about me?'

The door, which was ajar, was pushed farther open, and Isobel Meriden, her arms full of paper bags of groceries, came into the room.

She cried out, 'Holly—I thought you were in Portugal!' Dumping her parcels in a chair, she held out her arms. Holly got up, was embraced and kissed, then held at arm's length and inspected.

'You've bleached your hair,' Isobel stated. 'No, you haven't, it's the sun. But you *are* thinner. Do you eat enough alone in that flat of yours? Do you look after yourself properly? Do you ever do anything but open tins and drink too much strong coffee?'

She was very thin herself. But tins and strong coffee were not to blame. It was the feverish energy with which she worked at anything that caught her interest. She was never still. If it was true that to travel hopefully is better than to arrive, then, Holly had thought, Isobel must be one of the happiest mortals on earth, for she was only to be met with, and then usually very briefly, on the move from one place to another, probably pushing her sleeves up as she went, to cope more vigorously with what was ahead of her.

She had a thin, sharp-featured face, which would have been plain if it had not been as vividly alive as it was. Her big, slate-grey eyes were brilliant. Yet in an odd way they were always preoccupied, as if, by the time that they had come to rest on something, she was already beginning to think of something else. She nearly always dressed cheaply and badly, because she could not bring herself to spend money on herself, although she had always been lavish to her children. Only on very rare and special occasions, a plain and costly dress of great age would be dug out of some dark cupboard and she would appear in it, looking awkwardly yet haughtily distinguished, and somehow cheapening every other woman in the room.

The truth was, Isobel Meriden, in her way, was a very haughty woman, despising nearly everyone, including herself, for not coming up to some standard that she had set the human race. At the moment she was wearing a soiled, three-quarter-length waterproof over a tweed skirt that drooped at the back, a grey jersey and spotty, down-at-heel suede shoes.

'I just popped down to the shop for some things I'd forgotten,' she said. 'All the important things, as usual. I've had a hole in my head where my memory ought to be ever since all this worry started about Marcus. Rice, peppers, onions—because I bought chicken livers in Helsington this morning to make a risotto, and I only found after I'd got home that I'd run out of all the other things I needed. But our local shop's wonderful now, it keeps nearly everything. Self-service, too—oh, we're developing in Roydon Saint Agnes. I suppose I oughtn't to patronize the place actually, because it belongs to the sister of that awful Mrs Gargrave who's trying to get our poor Marcus into gaol, but there's nowhere else to go except back into Helsington. I suppose Kate's told you all about Marcus, Holly. Kate, where is he? He said they didn't need him in the theatre today. I should have thought he'd be here with you.'

'I don't know where he is,' Kate said. 'I haven't seen him.'

'But doesn't he know Holly's here?'

'I don't know,' Kate replied indifferently.

Isobel's eyes glinted excitedly. 'He'd hate not to know she's there. He adores her. But he can't know it, or he'd be here with you. Where *is* he?'

Kate shrugged her shoulders. 'Does it matter? You shouldn't worry about him so. It only annoys him.'

'But I can't help worrying,' Isobel said. 'I wish I knew where he's gone. Holly, you're staying to dinner, of course. Kate, darling, be a love and dump these things in the kitchen for me, because I want to telephone Judy and ask her to come too—there'll be enough to feed an army.'

Before Holly had had time to say that she could not stay, and that she was sure that Judy could not come either, because she was expecting that visit from Stephen Floyd, Isobel darted out of the room.

'It's all right, I'll tell her,' Kate said as she gathered up the parcels from the chair. 'As a matter of fact, she's probably forgotten by now she was going to telephone Judy. She really has got a hole in her head. The only thing she can think about is Marcus. I didn't tell her, but probably he's taken Loraine out somewhere. You'd think, after what she's done to him, that he'd have had enough of her, but he still seems to think he can talk her round. He's always been able to talk people round before. He can't believe it may not happen this time.'

With her long strides, she went out of the room.

Almost as soon as she had gone, Isobel came running back. She grasped Holly above the elbows with her thin, strong fingers.

'Holly, now you're here, you'll try to help us, won't you? See if you can get Marcus to talk to you. See if you can get at the truth. He won't talk to me any more. He shuts me out. So I don't know how I can help him, and he needs help so badly. Ben doesn't do anything. He never has. He's got his work. And Andrew's been away so long, he's out of touch. Anyway, he sort of intimidates Marcus. The elder brother, you know. And Kate wouldn't dream of letting anyone know she cares, though, of course, she does. So there's only me, and I seem just to antagonize Marcus when I try to get near him. So please help us if you get the chance—only I needn't have asked you, I know that, because of course you will.' She let go of Holly abruptly and turned back to the door. 'I wish I knew where he was. I know I shouldn't, but I worry whenever I don't know. I never used to, you know that. I liked the children to be as independent as possible. But these last few weeks I've felt as if I'm about going mad.'

She fled from the room again.

Left alone there, Holly wandered to the curved bay at the end of the room. Outside it was nearly dark. In the glass of the three tall windows, her own reflection walked towards her out of the invisible garden. Pale and faint against the dusk, three images of herself converged upon her. There were raindrops on the glass and the sound of a wind beginning to moan faintly.

The atmosphere in the house was so unlike anything that she had ever experienced there before that she was oddly at a loss, because for most of her life she had been as much at home here as at Cross Cottage, and more so than she had ever been in any of the London flats that she had briefly inhabited with her parents.

She thought about Marcus. How could she help him? Did she even want to help him, if it happened to be true that he had turned into the sort of boy who knocked down old men and kicked their ribs in? Giving a slight shiver, she turned away from the window.

She found herself face to face with Andrew, who had come into the room without her hearing him.

What happened to Holly then reached back to something that had happened to her much longer ago than the last time that she had seen Andrew, just before he left for Canada.

It had happened one day soon after she had come to Cross Cottage for the first time, when she was ten, and Andrew, a grown-up fifteen-year-old, had put his head into the playroom to see how the kids were treating the newcomer who had been sent to play with them. At once, at that moment, Holly had realized that she was looking at the most superb human being whom she had ever seen in her life. Something about him, she had no idea what, had instantly put him above and apart from everyone else whom she had ever known. Abruptly, from one moment to the next, without consideration or reservations, she had given her heart away, and for about the next five years had faithfully, ardently and undemandingly worshipped the ground he walked on.

Of course, he had known it, and allowing for some self-consciousness which had sometimes made him mildly cruel, particularly if other boys of his own age were around, he had been gratified by her adoration and had treated her passion gently. Really he had always been a very gentle boy and unusually tolerant for an adolescent of the emotions that can rend the hearts of the very young. When they happened to be alone together he had pretended to treat her as an equal, showing surprising patience in finding subjects that they could discuss, and on a few wonderful occasions had taken her with him, bicycling and swimming. But then he had gone to Cambridge, and Holly, growing older, had been forced to recognize that there were other girls in his life. Then he had gone to Canada, which had been a pain that had numbed her for a very long time, but still in her life there had begun to be other men. Andrew's image had grown dim. But now, for an instant, as they faced one another in the long drawing-room, the intervening years vanished and the grave-faced boy with whom she had so suddenly fallen in love was looking into the playroom again.

She said, 'Please don't say you thought I was in Portugal, Andrew. You knew if you wrote to me I'd come. And here I am. So tell me now, why did you write to me?'

## CHAPTER III

HE PUT HIS ARMS round her and kissed her. It was warm, friendly, and not at all intense. A let-down. But also a relief, because, where Andrew was concerned, some of the old numbness had never gone, and she was deeply scared of having life return to the deadened nerves.

'I never thought you'd come,' he said, 'but it's very good to see you.'

'You mean it wasn't important? You said it was. So I cancelled everything and came. I've always done everything you asked.'

'Oh God, then it had better be important, hadn't it?'

He gave her an affectionate smile. He had not changed much since she had seen him last. He looked a little leaner. His face looked tauter and was rather more like his mother's than Holly had ever noticed before. He had her colouring, her big, slate-grey eyes, her dark brown hair and pointed features. His movements had always been swift and restless, as hers were. But his eyes were without the evasive look that Isobel's always had, so that you never felt entirely sure that she was listening to you when you talked to her. Rather, Andrew's seemed to concentrate with unusual directness on anyone with whom he was talking. He was not as tall as Holly remembered. Naturally, for the imprint that he had left on her memory was of the big boy, a foot or so taller than she was herself, who had been nice to her long ago in the playroom, and since that time she had done a little catching up.

He went on, 'You see, Holly, it's just that it's four years since I was home last, and one of the things I was looking forward to most was seeing you again, and then it turned out you were abroad, so I wrote . . . I suppose I shouldn't have, but I didn't seriously think you'd come.'

'You knew I would.'

'I honestly didn't,' he said. 'For all I knew, you were hooked up with someone over there from whom there'd be no prying you loose.'

'But you've hardly written to me at all, all these years,' she said. 'About three letters, I think. So naturally I thought this meant something important.'

'So it does—to me.'

'I thought, from the way you wrote, you were in trouble of some sort.'

'Trouble? Oh yes, there's trouble.' With one of his rapid movements, he swung away from her towards the fireplace, where a log fire had been laid but not yet lit. 'Lots and lots of trouble.'

'About Marcus?'

'Marcus?' For an instant, she could have sworn, he was surprised. He had not been thinking of Marcus. But after a moment he said, 'Yes, of course, Marcus.'

'Isobel seems to think I can help, but I don't know how,' Holly said.

She had always called her own parents Mummy and Daddy, and had never wanted to call them anything else, but it would have sounded very odd to her in the Meriden family if any of them had ever done that to their parents.

'Well, you could always handle him, couldn't you?' Andrew said. 'But let's not talk about him now. He's a fool. He's going through a bad phase. A strange streak of violence seems to have come out in him which is going to give him a lot of grief if he doesn't grow out of it. And there's something in the atmosphere here too which is new since I went away. Sometimes I feel it's a sort of hate. Does that sound absurd to you? I feel they're all tied together by knots they'd like to break and can't. It makes me want to get away again as fast as I can.'

'How soon do you go?' Holly asked.

'I've got another fortnight.'

'Then I'm glad you wrote,' she said. 'I don't know what I'd have felt like if I'd found you'd been here and I'd missed you.'

'But I oughtn't to have spoilt your holiday. That wasn't fair, interrupting I don't know what.'

'You didn't interrupt anything special.'

'Is that the truth?'

'Yes, I was with some friends. Other students. We'd had about enough of each other by the time I left.'

He smiled at her and with that direct gaze of his on her face, seemed to forget that there was any need to go on talking.

She settled into one of the easy-chairs and picked up the glass of sherry that she had started earlier.

He said at once, 'Shall I top that up?' and went and fetched the bottle and filled the glass to the brim. 'Poor Isobel,' he went on. 'Incidentally, have you noticed how everyone keeps saying, "poor Isobel", and not "poor old man in the Sea Cave"? But she can't understand what's hit her. Yet she should. It's only the logical conclusion of the way she saw fit to bring us all up. We always had to be ourselves. If we felt aggressive, we weren't to suppress it, we were to work it out of our systems. The theory was, I suppose, that in the end there'd be none left to work out.

Unfortunately, it just happens that the supply of it in some people seems to be inexhaustible.'

'You seem to be taking for granted that Marcus is guilty,' Holly said.

'No, I'm not,' he retorted. 'Damn the subject, anyway. It's obsessive. If you spend a few days in this house, you'll find you can't talk about anything else. Tell me about Portugal.'

'It was hot, it was sunny, we swam and we looked at churches and pictures, and the food's nothing special, but we ate an awful lot of it, and the wine's indifferent, but we drank a good deal of that too, and the men are slender and elegant and the women are funny little dumpy people . . . But really, in a fortnight, one doesn't get to know anything at all. Tourism is the very opposite of travel, isn't it?'

'You did too much travelling in your youth,' he said. 'You're blasé.'

'Still, some day I'd like to travel properly,' she said. 'I mean to some of the places I really want to go to, not just to the places where they send oil men.'

'Let me warn you,' he said, 'all by oneself one gets lonely. I'd like to come back to England.'

'But just now you sounded as if you were sick of your home, not for it.'

'Oh no, that isn't so,' he said. 'I'm very fond of them all. It's just this atmosphere . . .'

'Do you think you will come back?'

'Some time, perhaps, if the chance comes up. But I don't want to keep on rattling round from one thing to another. I enjoy stability. Holly, what are you doing tomorrow?'

'Nothing special.'

'Could I pick you up after breakfast, and could we drive a long way, right out of this atmosphere, and talk about things that have nothing to do with what's been going on here? We've lots to talk about. All that's happened during four years. That should keep us busy.'

'I'd love that,' she said.

'Suppose I call for you about half past nine.'

She nodded. 'Only perhaps I ought to make sure Judy hasn't any plans for me. She probably hasn't, but I'd better make sure. I'll ring you up later this evening, shall I? It's time I went now. Judy's expecting me home.'

'Right. I'll drive you home then. Come along.'

They went out together.

In the hall they met Kate, who protested that they could not leave her to drink alone, but Holly insisted that she had to go. The car was at the door, where Isobel had left it after her drive to the village shop. The evening had become very dark because of the heavy, low clouds that covered the sky. Thin, steady rain was falling.

The drive to Cross Cottage was down the long, winding farm drive, which emerged on to the road about a hundred yards from the crossroads. It took only a few minutes. The windscreen wipers, swinging from side to side, left clear arcs on the rain-blurred glass. The wet surface of the drive, between dark banks of laurel and rhododendron, took on a look of high polish in the beam of the headlights.

'If it rains tomorrow, we'll go all the same, shall we?' Andrew said.

'Oh yes,' Holly agreed. 'What's a little rain?'

'But perhaps it'll be fine. What shall we do, have lunch in a pub, or shall I ask Isobel for some food?'

'If it looks fine, let's have a picnic. But Andrew, tell me something. When I said to you I thought, from the way you wrote, that you were in trouble of some sort, and you agreed you were, and I thought you meant Marcus and you agreed you did . . .'

'Well?' he asked.

'Well, I had a feeling it wasn't really Marcus you'd been thinking about at all. I had a feeling you were rather surprised at the way I jumped to that conclusion.'

'Did you?'

'Are you in some other sort of trouble?'

'Absolutely none.'

'Are you sure?' It was silly to press on with it, because it was obvious that even if she was right, he had made up his mind not to talk about the matter, and when Andrew, in his quiet fashion, made up his mind, there was never much that anyone could do about it.

'I'm sorry I gave you the idea I was in any trouble,' he said. 'It didn't occur to me you were asking me about myself. There's trouble in the family, of course—this Marcus affair.'

'Nothing else?'

'Isn't that enough to be going on with?'

'Oh, well, I suppose I was wrong.'

'Any time I'm in trouble, you'll be the first to hear.' He stopped the car at the door of Cross Cottage, and as she was about to get out, held her back and kissed her again. Once more, it was only a brief, almost diffident kiss, and once more, in its way, was disappointing. 'I promise,' he said.

Holly looked thoughtfully into his face in the light that had come on in the car as she opened the door and saw that his smile was a little fixed, and that his direct, bright eyes were blanker than usual. She decided that she did not believe his promise.

Standing on the doorstep of the cottage, she watched as he backed the car to the crossroads, swung it round there and disappeared up the road to the farm, then she turned to go in. She was thinking about how difficult it seemed to be to pick up the threads of an old relationship after a period as long as four years, particularly a relationship that had been as charged with emotion as the one between herself and Andrew. Somehow this evening had all been different from what she had expected when she had come charging back from Portugal at Andrew's casual request. Andrew himself had been far more subdued than she remembered him, though perhaps, except in occasional moods of wildness and excitement, he had always been rather self-contained. But Holly was thinking now how she herself did not feel like the person she had been when he went away and that in some ways it appeared to be far less complicated to start up new relationships with people whom one had never met before than to reach back into the past and come up with something that one was sure meant something. However, perhaps she would learn more about herself tomorrow. She opened the cottage door.

Because she had been so engrossed in her own feelings, it was only then that it struck her as odd that apparently there was not a single light on inside. Vaguely she had noticed while she was still outside that there were no lights in any of the windows, but she had not paid this much attention. If Judy had gone out, she supposed, she would probably have left a note somewhere, telling Holly when to expect her back. She pressed the light-switch by the front door, crossed the small hall, went to the door of the sitting-room, reached inside and pressed the light-switch there.

It was in the instant before she did that that she had the first sense of something amiss. A cold draught was blowing into her face, when it should not have been. The draught came from the french window, which was wide open. The curtains were flapping in the wind and the sound of rain-drops was pattering on the polished floor inside. It did not seem right.

But that faint forewarning was no preparation for what Holly saw as the light came on. Judy was lying in the middle of the room, a room which was in chaos. Drawers had been pulled open, books swept from the shelves, cushions thrown on the floor. There was the dreadfulness of raging violence in the place, like a rank, bestial smell. Judy's eyes stared up without blinking straight into the light that Holly had just switched on. There was blood thickening in her grey hair and down one side of her bruised, purple, pulpy-looking face. Holly knew that she was dead and she began to scream and scream.

It took her a moment to realize that those screams were her own. She had clapped her hands over her ears to shut out the horrible noise before she discovered that it was she who was making it. She stopped at once then. Blank silence followed.

Advancing into the room, she knelt down beside Judy. She touched her cooling flesh here and there and took her hand. How long she stayed there, rigid with shock and fear, she did not know. It might have been two minutes, it might have been ten. But at last she got up and proceeded immediately to do several things that she ought not to have done, because, on the scene of a murder, of course, one is supposed not to touch anything. She closed the french window and locked and bolted it, shutting out the rain and the chill. Then she drew all the curtains in the room. These actions were instinctive. She did not say to herself that if the monster who had done this to Judy were still out there, she did not want him peering in at her, alone, like Judy, in the cottage. Holly only knew that she had to protect herself from the darkness and the wet night.

Next she went to the front door and locked and bolted it also, then went into the kitchen to the back door and did the same there. As she crossed the kitchen she noticed absently that Judy had washed the tea-things that they had used that afternoon and left them in the rack to dry. Also Holly noticed some roses on the draining-board beside the sink, together with a pair of scissors and an empty vase. She went next to the study. The telephone was there on the desk. She pressed the switch of the table-lamp so that she could see to dial 999.

As she dialled the magic numbers that were certain to bring help, she found that she could not think of words in which to describe what had happened and why she needed help. But a surprisingly intelligent sergeant seemed to make sense of her ramblings and told her to stay where she was and that someone would be there directly. Holly wondered what 'directly' meant, ten minutes, twenty, half an hour?

Putting the telephone back on its stand, she dropped into the chair at the desk and began to shake. Like the sitting-room, the room was in a terrible mess, drawers pulled out, papers strewn everywhere. That in itself was frightening and horrifying. She was still shaking helplessly and was feeling deathly cold when someone pounded on the front door with the knocker.

The incredible efficiency of the police bewildered her. How could they possibly have got here so soon? It beat Z Cars. But perhaps, she thought, her time-sense had got out of gear and she had been sitting there for much longer than it seemed. Pushing herself up out of the chair, she went to the door, and only, at the last moment, as she reached up to pull back the bolt, felt a wild surge of panic so that she froze where she stood.

The knocker sounded again.

She called out, 'Who's there?'

'Stephen,' a man's voice answered. Then, as she still did not move and did not speak again, he asked anxiously, 'Judy, is anything wrong?'

Holly began to come to herself, pulled back the bolt, turned the key and opened the door.

When he saw her face, Stephen Floyd exclaimed, 'Good God, what's happened?'

She thought that he had been struck by her look of dazed fright and it was not until she happened to catch sight of her face in a mirror presently that she found that there was a bright smear of blood down one cheek. She must have touched Judy's battered face and then her own.

Standing aside, Holly gestured at the door of the sitting-room.

He went to it quickly. It was only then that she realized that he had not come to the cottage alone. A small woman in a mackintosh and short gum boots had been standing in the road behind him.

She said pleasantly, 'You must be Holly Dunthorne.

Stephen told me about giving you a lift this afternoon. I thought I'd come along with him now and help him and Judy with my invaluable advice. I'm Lisa Chard.'

She advanced into the light that fell through the open door.

She was small, not much over five foot one or two. Her hair was a carroty red and short and straight. She had full cheeks, a short, pert nose, a wide mouth and a very slight cast in her eye which gave a curious, ambiguous depth to her glance. The rest of her seemed to be all waterproof and boots.

She did not react to the sight of Holly's face as Stephen had, but acted as if to be bloodsmeared were quite normal in any young woman. Apologizing for the boots, she rubbed them on the doormat.

'They aren't really muddy,' she said. Her voice was low-pitched, with the huskiness of the heavy smoker about it. 'It isn't raining as hard as I thought. Judy!' She raised her voice to call Judy's name and walked towards the sitting-room.

Holly came to life then and began to say, 'Don't . . .'

But Lisa Chard had already reached the door of the sitting-room and was looking in.

She stood still for only a moment, then she walked on into the room. She said nothing. Holly felt that she ought to follow her, but at that moment she could not have taken a step in that direction for anything in the world. Almost immediately Lisa Chard reappeared, with Stephen Floyd following her.

He asked, 'Have you rung the police?'

Holly nodded.

'What happened?' He looked far paler than the woman.

She said, 'Don't badger the child, Stephen. She'll have to go through it all when the police come. What she needs is a stiff drink. I wonder if Judy has any brandy in the house. Do you know, Holly?'

Holly did not, but Stephen did, and pointing towards the sitting-room, said, 'She generally kept her drinks in the corner cupboard in there.'

Lisa Chard turned and walked back into the room, re-emerging with a bottle of brandy in her hand.

'Come in here and sit down,' she said, leading the way into the study. 'God, what a mess. I wonder what they were looking for—or was it just destructiveness for its own sake? No, nothing's been smashed. Stephen, get some glasses. I expect you'll find them in the kitchen.'

Obediently, he went, returning with glasses which he put on the desk.

Lisa Chard thrust Holly into the chair where she had been sitting when they arrived, filled the glasses, put one in Holly's hand and herself sat down on a corner of the desk. Her mackintosh had fallen open and showed a plain jersey dress inside, which, Holly knew, because she had one just like it, had come from Marks and Spencer's. Pinned to the dress was a brooch which sparkled so brilliantly when it caught the light that the stones in it could not have been anything but real diamonds. Lisa was a sturdily built, though small-boned woman of about forty, with no make-up on her face and with very short, unpolished nails on her short strong fingers.

The brandy immediately made Holly want to talk. She heard herself doing it without feeling responsible for what she was saying. That did not seem to matter. These two people who had rescued her from the awful emptiness of the house felt like her best friends, to whom she could say anything.

'I'd been to the Meridens,' she said. 'Judy said she wanted a bath. She'd been gardening all the afternoon . . . You know, she didn't have that bath. She's in the same clothes as she was when I arrived here . . . And she wanted to do some cooking too, so she suggested I should go over to see Kate, as I always used to when I came here from school. I often used to come here for the holidays, because my parents were generally abroad and they couldn't always afford to have me flown out to where they were. They're in Australia at the moment. So I went over to the Meridens and stayed a bit, then I came back, and there she was.'

'Just a minute,' Stephen Floyd said as Holly paused to drink some more of the comforting brandy. 'How did you get in?'

'By the front door,' she said. 'It wasn't locked. It never is, except at night, or if Judy goes out. The french window in the sitting-room wasn't locked either. Actually it was wide open and it was raining in, so I shut it and bolted it and drew the curtains, and bolted the front and the back doors too.'

'You say the curtains weren't drawn when you got here?' he said.

Lisa exclaimed impatiently, 'Don't keep on at her, Stephen. Let her tell her story in her own way, or not at all, if she doesn't want to.'

A muscle in his cheek twitched slightly as if he did not like her authoritative tone. He muttered, 'It's just that it might be important. The police are going to want to know when it all happened, and if the curtains weren't drawn when Holly came in, then it was probably before it got dark. And if the french window was wide open, then it was probably before the rain started. And if only you'd let me come here when I said I ought to, it might never have happened at all.'

'If I'd *let* you . . .?' Lisa said, raising her eyebrows.

'I told you Judy was expecting me,' he said. 'I asked you, what's the good of going round to advise her about that room she wants to build on when it's pitch dark? Didn't I say that?'

'And didn't I say, "Have another drink before you go", and weren't you very willing to have it, and then another? Don't talk as if I could have stopped you coming if you'd wanted to. You aren't a child.' She turned back to Holly. 'Don't worry, Holly, they'll soon find out who did it. In a place like this they're bound to do it quite easily. It was probably some toughs from Helsington. Someone's sure to have seen something suspicious. If that's any comfort to you.'

'But why did it happen?' Holly demanded, and stared at the little woman as if in her wisdom she would be able to tell her. 'What did they do it for?'

'It looks to me like a fairly straightforward robbery,' Lisa said. 'Perhaps they thought the house was empty. Judy may have been in the garden and not heard them when they knocked to see if anyone was in. Then she may have come in and caught them, and somebody lost his head and did something worse than he intended.'

'Perhaps she'd gone out to the back to finish picking the apples,' Holly said. 'When I got here in the afternoon she was on the step-ladder, picking apples. I interrupted her. So perhaps she went back to get a few more. Or perhaps she simply went out to pick some roses. There are some on the draining-board by the sink, with an empty vase. You know, I think that's when he came. I'd just gone to the Meridens, and I think Judy went out to pick some flowers for my room—she used always to put some there if she knew I was coming—and she'd just got them into the kitchen and was going to arrange them when something interrupted her. Someone knocking at the door, or someone coming into the house. Otherwise she'd never have left the roses there without putting them in water.'

At the thought of Judy picking the roses for her room, tears spilled out of Holly's eyes, the first tears that she had shed since she had come into the house and found Judy. They blurred the image of Lisa Chard, sitting on the edge of the desk, swinging a foot that did not quite touch the floor, and sipping brandy.

'Of course, there may be a maniac around,' Lisa remarked in a tone of calm detachment. 'Somebody nobody suspects of being crazy, except perhaps his mother. Mothers have a way of knowing things and keeping their mouths shut. I'm thinking of a case some years ago of some village boy who murdered an old woman who'd always been good to him, simply because she'd offended him over some trivial thing, and his mother covered up for him as long as she could, then admitted at last that he'd always been a little strange. It could be something like that, perhaps. Judy was involved in lots of things, she met all kinds of people. I suppose one of them could have been mad. A person would have to be mad to murder Judy.'

'Only isn't mad an unfashionable word these days?' Stephen said drily. 'We're mentally disturbed, or we have pathological personalities, but we don't go mad any more. A cheering thought, perhaps. Holly, how long is it since you last saw Judy? I mean before this afternoon.'

'Some months,' Holly said. 'She came and stayed with me in London for a few days—in May, I think it was.'

'And she didn't say anything then that suggested she was afraid of anybody, or worrying about anything?'

'Can't you stop badgering Holly with questions?' Lisa broke in before Holly could answer. 'I'm sorry, Holly. He's probably only doing it so that we don't sit around in an awful silence until the police get here, but he shouldn't do it.'

'If so,' he said, 'can't you leave it to Holly to tell me so herself?'

Lisa shot him a faintly cross-eyed glance, which Holly found unreadable. 'All right, I will. Holly, just tell us to mind our own business, if you want to.'

In a way that was just what Holly wanted to do. She had begun to find Lisa's personality too strong for her. A few moments ago, Holly had started to feel that she was being pushed in some direction in which she was not sure that she wanted to go. She did not want to form opinions yet about what had happened, or why it had happened. In a way, she simply did not want to think at all. It seemed to her that she could remember every detail of that awful room as an abstract pattern printed on her mind in hideous colours, but she did not want to start struggling yet after the significance of the pattern.

At the same time, she had started puzzling about the relationship between these two people. She could feel antagonism between them, and if Stephen Floyd had not spoken of Lisa Chard that afternoon as his friend and been going to see her and apparently spent the time since then with her, Holly would have felt almost certain that they disliked one another intensely. At the least, there was acute tension between them, which jarred her sharply as she became aware of it, because of the more desperate state of tension that she was in herself.

Lisa went on, 'A thing we ought to be thinking about is where you're going to spend the night, Holly. You can't possibly stay here. Would you like to stay with me? You'd be very welcome—though I expect you'd sooner stay with the Meridens, as they're old friends. Would you? Why don't you telephone them now and tell them what's happened? Or shall I do it for you? But I meant what I said, if you'd like to come to me. My spare room's always ready.'

Of course, Holly would have preferred to spend the night with the Meridens rather than with a stranger, but she felt that it might sound an ungrateful thing to say. However, just then the door-knocker sounded again, so she did not have to decide how to answer, and this time it was the police, and all at once the cottage was filled to bursting with big, busy men with loud voices, tramping feet, note-books, cameras, flash bulbs and questions that they wanted answered.

The man in charge was Detective-Superintendent Ditteridge, a tall man who, immediately on entering the cottage, gave his head a serious bump against one of the low beams in the hall ceiling and, as he rubbed his forehead, had the self-control to smile and say, 'Everyone who comes in here does that at least once, I suppose. Now what's all this about?'

## CHAPTER IV

HE WAS AN AGEING MAN, with close-cropped, bristly grey hair, a long, lined face with a jutting promontory of a chin, restless, light brown eyes and an air of good-natured interest in the scene before him. But when you met his eyes, Holly found, they were not really good-natured, but singularly cold. It was as if he felt that he had looked on more than enough of human evil in his time and had no intention of letting his private emotions be unpleasantly disturbed by it. When presently he wanted to question Holly, they settled down in the kitchen, since there were no signs there, as there were in the other ground-floor rooms, that the killer had been in it. The roses, wilting, were still on the draining-board. Holly pointed them out to him and told him what she thought about them. He nodded and went on to ask her almost the same questions as Lisa Chard and Stephen Floyd had asked earlier. When had Holly arrived in Roydon Saint Agnes? What had her aunt been doing? What mood had she been in? When had Holly gone to the Meridens and when had she returned? How had she got into the house? Just what had she done then? She had shut and bolted all the doors and drawn the curtains, had she . . .?

Holly said that she was sorry about doing that and he answered, 'Natural, perfectly natural. Wouldn't have been nice to see a face looking in at you. I'd have done the same myself. Now did Miss Dunthorne say anything to you about expecting any visitor this evening?'

'Only Mr Floyd,' Holly said.

'Oh, she was expecting him?'

'Yes, to give her some advice about some alterations she was thinking of having done to the cottage.'

'What time did she expect him?'

'I don't think any special time. I think she just told me he was going to drop in some time.'

'You'd think it would be before dark.'

'I suppose so, yes.'

'Yet according to his own story and Miss Chard's, he only arrived here a little while ago.'

'Yes, that's right.'

'Did he explain the delay?'

Holly shook her head. 'I think he just didn't notice how late it was getting.'

Mr Ditteridge's gaze was wandering around the kitchen while they talked, but now it came back to Holly's face. 'We've found something rather curious, Miss Dunthorne, which I don't expect you noticed because of its being dark and raining when you got back from visiting your friends, and because you were upset and frightened. There are signs that there was some sort of struggle in the garden.'

'In the *garden*?' She looked at him without comprehension.

'Yes,' he said. 'If you'd looked outside before you shut the french window of the sitting-room, you'd have seen that some of that garden furniture on the terrace there was overturned. The table and two chairs. And there are the remains of some broken glasses on the ground. I can't tell you yet how many glasses, but at least one of them was a tumbler, and one was a cut-glass sherry glass. There's a beer bottle on the ground too that didn't break. Did Miss Dunthorne drink beer, or do you think she'd have been the one who was drinking sherry?'

'Probably the sherry,' Holly said.

'Well, there may be fingerprints that will tell us for sure, in spite of the rain,' he said. 'In any case, it's reasonable to suppose she sat out there having a drink with someone. And then something happened. Something resulted in that table and those chairs getting overturned and the glasses broken, and sent Miss Dunthorne running into the house with someone after her . . .' He paused, giving a little tug at his jutting chin. 'You understand, I'm not sure that's how it was. I'm just trying to reconstruct what might have happened. Perhaps the person or persons she sat out there having drinks with didn't murder her. Someone else could have come in later. But what's sure is that something happened on the terrace that resulted in that furniture getting upset and the glasses smashed. So we need to know pretty badly, don't we, who the person or persons may have been?'

'I don't think it was anyone she was expecting,' Holly said, 'or she'd have said something about it to me before I went to the Meridens.'

'There's another thing in the garden,' he said. 'There's a step-ladder and a basket of apples out under that apple tree on the lawn. Would Miss Dunthorne have left them there, would you say, till after it was dark and started to rain? I mean, was she a careless person, who'd maybe forget them and leave them out all night, or do you think she'd normally have brought them in?'

'I think she'd have brought them in,' Holly said.

'But suppose she was interrupted by something that took her mind right off them.'

'Yes,' Holly said, 'I see.'

'So how it looks,' he said, 'is that when you left here to visit your friends—that was about six-fifteen, you think, don't you?—she went out into the garden to pick those roses for your room, brought them in, got out the vase, and just then someone came to the house—say about six-thirty—someone she knew well enough to ask him to stay for a drink, and they had the drink together on the terrace. And then things went wrong. There was a quarrel, violence, and she ran into the house and whoever it was followed her in and killed her. He used a bronze vase to do it, a Japanese-looking thing shaped sort of like a lily. Do you know it?'

'Oh yes, it's always been there on top of a bookcase.'

'So he didn't come prepared to do murder, he just used what came to hand. And then he searched the room, or else wanted us to think he searched the room. It could be, you see, that once he'd killed her, he thought he'd try to make it look like a case of robbery, so he turned the place upside down before he left.'

Holly's eyes were smarting with fatigue. She shut them, trying to visualize the scene that he had described to her, the drinks, the friendly talk, the quarrel, the upsetting of the garden furniture, the horrible end. But at once the darkness began to spin round, making her feel sick. It did not help her that, having been travelling since dawn, she had not had a square meal all day. She felt weak and hollow inside, although quite without hunger.

'I don't understand, you're talking as if she were killed by someone she knew quite well,' she said. 'But there'd have to be a reason for that, and I can't see how there can have been a reason. Not with Judy. Of course, I know awful things happen without any reason—any reason a normal person can understand. Is that the sort of thing you mean? I don't think she'd have suspected anything abnormal in anyone she knew unless it was fearfully obvious. I don't think she ever managed to believe in evil . . .' Her voice dried up miserably.

'About Mr Floyd,' he said.

'Well?'

'What do you know of Miss Dunthorne's relations with him?'

'*Relations*?' Holly wondered vaguely if he had some idea that Judy might have been having a love-affair with Stephen Floyd, which struck her as about as ludicrous a suggestion as she had heard for a long time.

'Were they on good terms?' he asked.

'Oh, reasonably, I think, or she wouldn't have wanted him to make the alterations to the cottage, would she?'

'And you can't think of any enemies she may have had?'

'Oh no.'

'Now what about valuables in the cottage? Money? Jewellery?'

Holly shook her head. It occurred to her that somehow some monstrous mistake had been made and that she and Mr Ditteridge were not talking about the same person. Perhaps he had somehow been sent out to investigate the wrong murder case. Perhaps soon some other policeman would appear, who would begin to ask her questions about the Judy whom she had known, the woman who had really existed, not the imaginary figure whom this man seemed bent on creating.

But for the present all that happened was that Mr Ditteridge took Holly again through almost all the questions that he had already asked her, then wanted her to go up to Judy's bedroom and look into her small jewel-case, which she had kept in a drawer of her dressing-table, and tell him if anything appeared to be missing.

There was no disorder upstairs. The murderer had either found what he wanted downstairs or had given up the search without going up to the bedrooms. So far as Holly could tell, nothing was missing from the jewel-case. Judy had never had much jewellery. She had had a few rings and brooches and one or two pairs of ear-rings which she had inherited from her mother, all of such stones as opals, garnets and amethysts, and not much else.

Her handbag had been on a chair in the sitting-room, near her body. Mr Ditteridge brought it out of the sitting-room and showed it to Holly. The bag had been emptied on to the chair, he told her, but the money that had been in it had not been taken. There were seven pound notes and some small change. Holly nodded at it and said that that seemed to her about normal. Judy had never kept much money in the house. She had paid for most things by cheque. After that the superintendent let Holly go, advising her in his kindly voice, though with his gaze as remote as ever, to make herself a cup of tea. She said that she would, but in fact, as soon as he had rejoined the other men in the sitting-room, she went to the study, picked up the telephone and dialled the Meridens' number.

It was Isobel who answered. Her cheerful voice threw Holly into a state of confusion. She had somehow forgotten that, whoever answered, she would have to describe what had happened here. It seemed to her that everybody must already know about it. Something of such magnitude could not possibly have happened without its instantly becoming known everywhere. She had only been thinking of asking if she could stay the night.

She had said only two words when Isobel interrupted, 'Oh, Holly dear, it's you, isn't it? I expect it's Kate you want. Hold on a minute, I'll call her—'

'No!' Holly exclaimed. 'Not Kate. I mean, not specially. An awful thing's happened, Isobel, and I wanted to ask you—'

Again Isobel broke in, 'But I've just got the chicken livers ready to fry, darling, and everything else is ready too. I'm so sorry, but I simply must get back to the kitchen. I'll call Kate—hold on a moment.'

Holly heard her raised voice calling, 'Kate!'

The telephone was firmly taken out of Holly's grasp by Lisa Chard.

'Isobel,' she said swiftly and distinctly, 'will you listen a moment? Are you there? . . . Yes, well, listen, it's important. This is Lisa. I'm with Holly at Cross Cottage. She got home from your cottage and found Judy dead . . . Yes, I said *dead*. Murdered . . . What's that ?. . . Yes, I said *murdered*. Someone broke in and killed Judy and tore the place apart. And luckily Stephen and I happened to drop in, or Holly would have been all alone till the police came. The place is full of police now. And Holly was ringing up to ask if she could spend the night with you, because obviously she can't stay here. I said she was welcome to come to me, but naturally she'd sooner be with people she knows . . .' She paused and a puzzled expression crossed her face. 'Isobel!' she said more urgently. 'Isobel . . .?' Then she slowly put the telephone down. 'If that isn't the damnedest thing! She simply rang off. Didn't say a thing after

I said the word murder, just held on a moment, then simply rang off. I've always thought there was something the matter with that woman. She's really unbalanced. Shall I ring up again and hope we get one of the others?'

'No, let's leave it for now,' Holly said. 'She's always in such a hurry, rushing from one thing to another, she probably just didn't wait to answer you. She may be in the car already, dashing round here.'

But it was Ben Meriden who arrived about five minutes later.

A constable opened the door to him, then brought him to the study. Ben stood in the doorway, looking massive and curiously threatening in his simian way. His shoulders were hunched, with his long arms hanging straight and heavy at his sides, his head thrust forward and his gaze moving swiftly from one face to another.

'Is this true?' he demanded. 'Judy's dead?'

Mr Ditteridge, emerging once more from the sitting-room, answered, 'Yes, that's true, Mr Meriden.'

'Murdered? Did my wife get it right? Murdered?'

'Unquestionably. She was battered to death with a bronze vase in her sitting-room.'

Ben drew a long breath and his wandering gaze fastened on Lisa's face.

'I didn't believe Isobel,' he said. 'I told her she must have misunderstood what you said, Lisa. What are you doing here—you and Stephen?'

'We happened to drop in,' Lisa said. 'Judy was expecting Stephen to come and give her some advice about that room of hers she wanted to build out over the garage. Actually, it would have been too late for that. It was dark already. I don't know why we didn't notice how time was passing. But we thought we'd come all the same and explain.'

'Explain what?' Ben asked.

'Apologize, then, if it's any business of yours, Ben,' Stephen said with an edge on his voice. 'Now I wish to God I'd come earlier, when I promised. A lot earlier.'

'But you were with Lisa,' Ben said, his eyes still on her face. 'And you find it's difficult to get away from her if she wants to keep you, don't you, Stephen?'

'Yes, he was with me,' Lisa said, 'so he has an alibi, and so have I, which always may come in convenient. Have you an alibi, Ben dear?'

Something about her had subtly altered since Ben had come into the room. It was very strange. Holly could make nothing of it. Lisa seemed to have become quietly, elusively feline. She had become very still as if she were waiting for something. At the same time she seemed to have made her old waterproof fit her differently. If in itself it had not become elegant, it seemed to drape her in a way which suggested that what it covered was supremely so. It was a kind of display which seemed to confuse Ben, for after a moment he looked away from her and asked Mr Ditteridge, 'How long do you want to keep Miss Dunthorne here?'

'I don't see why she need stay at all,' he answered, 'so long as we know where to get hold of her if we need her.'

'In fact, we're probably all horribly in the way,' Lisa said. 'Would you like us to leave, Superintendent?'

'If you'll be in your home, Miss Chard, where perhaps I can call in later,' he said.

'Yes, and Mr Floyd will be with me for a while.'

Stephen began to say that he'd thought of returning to Helsington, but she interrupted him, 'You've had nothing to eat, Stephen. Come home and have an omelette. Then, if the superintendent wants you, he'll know where to find you. Ben, take Holly home and give her something to eat and put her to bed. She looks about ready to cave in.'

'Now everyone knows exactly what he's got to do,' Stephen said. 'We've been given our instructions. Superintendent, why don't you ask Miss Chard to solve your murder for you? It would save you so much trouble.'

Lisa's face suddenly blazed with astonishing rage.

'Stephen! Have you forgotten what this child's been through today? Will you be quiet?'

'Child?' he said. His bony face looked haggard in the bright strip-lighting attached to the kitchen ceiling. 'Holly's very grown-up, haven't you noticed? I shouldn't be surprised if she's the most grown-up person present. But I'm sorry, Holly, if I've said anything to worry you. It's just that Lisa's serene belief in her own wisdom brings out the worst in me. I think she has a knack of bringing out the worst in most people. Just see she doesn't start on you. It's so painless to begin with, so pleasant . . .'

Ben took a swift step forward. Then he stood still.

'Come along, Holly,' he said, 'let's go.'

They could not go soon enough for Holly. She hated the atmosphere that had suddenly developed in the room, as well as being utterly bewildered by it. In leaving, she almost forgot her suitcase. When she remembered it, Ben went upstairs for it, then they went out through the rainy darkness together, past the police cars and a little way along the road to where he had left his car. Neither of them spoke at all as they drove to the crossroads, turned right, drove on the short distance to the Meridens' gate, turned into the drive, then stopped.

They stopped so suddenly and unexpectedly that Holly was thrown forward in her seat. Ben was sitting staring ahead of him, looking wholly helpless. There was nothing there to stare at. Then he crossed his arms on the wheel in front of him and dropped his head on to them, hiding his face. His big body began to tremble.

'Ben—' Holly heard her own voice sounding thin and young and inadequate. She put a hand on his shoulder.

He winced away from her touch as if it burned him. But then he lifted his head and looked at her with a grimace on his face which he probably thought was a smile.

'I'm sorry, Holly, just give me a moment,' he said. There were tears in his eyes which he brushed away with the back of his hand. They were both silent for a little while. Then he went on, 'Think it strange, do you, that I should do this? Well, let me tell you something I haven't told anyone since I told Isobel all about it before we were married. She and I were once lovers.'

Holly felt hopelessly at sea. 'You and Lisa?'

He swore, as if her name were something obscene.

'Judy—I'm talking about Judy!' he said. 'I was in love with Judy. She was a beautiful girl, incredibly beautiful. Perhaps you can't imagine it, but she was lovely and vital. She was—oh, wonderful. We meant to get married. We would have if she'd had an ounce of faith in me. But she hadn't. Because I couldn't make money by my work, she thought I was just wasting my time. And Isobel had faith. Bless her, she had faith. And it's all very long ago, so long I'd never have dreamt poor Judy's death could do anything to me. It was before you were even born, Holly—think of that! But something in me just now is hurting like hell. All of a sudden those days feel as if they were only yesterday. Does one ever forget anything? Oh God, why can't one forget?'

Holly wished that he would drive on. She felt that she had just been given a glimpse of something that she ought never to have known. Judy must always have taken great pains that Holly should never know it, for that there had ever been anything between Judy and Ben Meriden was something that had never entered Holly's head. Come to think of it, and how absurd and childish it seemed now, it had never occurred to her that Judy had ever been in love with anybody.

But as Ben did not drive on, but only sat there with that indrawn look on his face that people have when they are thinking deeply about the past, Holly said, 'Wasn't it difficult for you, living so near to one another?'

He started slightly. 'What? Oh yes, at first, I suppose. I hardly remember. That's odd, isn't it? I remember hardly anything about our breaking up. It's the earlier time that's suddenly come back to me now, the time when we were still in love and hopeful and very happy. Can you imagine that Judy was once a very desirable woman, Holly? Perhaps to you she was always just middle-aged, but in those days . . . Of course, her parents ate her up, once your father went away, and she had such a sense of duty, she never left home, and I suppose that's why she never married anyone else. She should have. It was a great waste. She had all the qualities that should have given her a happy marriage, passion, generosity, understanding.'

'I don't think she was wasted,' Holly said. 'She had a great many friends.'

'What's friendship?' Ben asked flatly. 'It's only the odd meeting from time to time, the occasional helping hand held out, a limited sort of trust . . . No, don't listen to me. I've never had friends. I don't seem to have had time for it. I don't really know what it's all about. Judy and I stayed friends of a sort, I suppose. And Judy and Isobel were friends, and I think that's what made things come right between the three of us. Anyway, after a time, Judy and I seemed to be getting along as if we'd never been anything but good neighbours, and Isobel was never jealous. And that's what it's been like for years . . .' He stopped and brushed his hand across his eyes again. 'Well, that's over. I'm sorry to have inflicted it on you, Holly. If you could manage not to mention it to the others, I'd be grateful.'

'What do you take me for?' Holly asked.

'Sorry—that was something I shouldn't have said, isn't it? Of course you won't mention it.' He started the car again and drove on to the house.

As soon as they reached it the door was flung open and Isobel erupted out of it. She came running to the car before Ben or Holly had had time to get out. She had on an apron over her jersey and skirt and her brown hair was wild, as if she had been combing it with her fingers.

'Holly, what *is* this?' she cried. 'Is it true? Murder? . . .

I didn't take it in properly. That woman, Lisa, talking—I didn't really listen. But Ben was there and heard it and jumped in the car and shot off before I'd found out anything. It *is* true, isn't it, and I was stupid? Come in now. You're as white as a sheet. Do you feel ill? Shall I call Dr James?'

The rain splashed on their heads as they crossed to the doorway. Andrew and Kate were there, and behind them a tall figure which it took Holly a moment to recognize as Marcus. He had not been nearly so tall when she had seen him last.

'She's perfectly all right,' Ben said, following Isobel and Holly into the house. 'She's just had the most horrible experience of her life and she's standing up under it pretty well.'

He seemed quite composed himself now, as if he had never had those few minutes of breakdown in the car.

'But perhaps a sedative . . .' Isobel said. 'Not that I believe in all these pills, you know. Everyone takes pills for everything nowadays. They don't seem able to face any kind of experience without its appropriate pill. I don't approve. But I keep various things upstairs. Old James keeps giving them to me for my insomnia, but I never take them.'

Andrew said, 'My guess is, she needs a square meal.'

'Food!' Isobel exclaimed, her face brightening, because this was something she understood. 'Of course! She'll have had nothing but that awful aeroplane stuff all day. What a pity the risotto got spoilt. It was your telephone call did it, Holly. I lost my head and let it burn and had to throw it away. We've been eating scrambled eggs. I'll make some for you, shall I? And there's some good soup—I'll just warm it up again—and I'll make some coffee, or will that keep you awake? I'll make some anyway. The rest of us can drink it.'

All the time that she was talking, she looked as if she were thinking of something else, something, whatever it was, that frightened her. Her thin face was even more pinched than usual. As she fled away to the kitchen, Kate took Holly by the arm and guided her into the drawing-room and pushed her into a chair.

The fire had been lit and was blazing cheerfully up the chimney. Kate went automatically to the tray of drinks and began to pour one.

'No thanks, if that's for me,' Holly said. 'I've already had some brandy.'

'Then have some more,' Kate said. 'It'll help to make you sleep.'

'No, thank you.' Holly was already slightly fuddled by the brandy that Lisa had given her and as she sat there in the chair by the warm fire, her head felt like a ton weight, her eyelids were trying to close of themselves and the room looked dim and distant. She supposed that it was a mixture of shock and simple fatigue, but she felt as if she might topple over unconscious at any moment.

But Kate poured out some brandy and put it down at Holly's elbow.

A hand appeared from behind her and picked up the glass.

'If you don't want it, I'll drink it,' Marcus said. 'I need it, if nobody else does.'

Coming round her chair, he stood in front of her.

She was startled at how very tall he was, and he was broad to go with it. Beautifully proportioned, she thought, looking up at him. She had been right when she told Stephen Floyd that Marcus was beautiful and special. Those were the right words for him. The golden hair that curled up at his neck, the glowing skin, the wide-spaced, mild blue eyes, the soft, wide mouth, the vulnerable air, all added up to something which, if she had been a painter, she thought, would have driven her crazy. She would have had to try to capture it, to possess it. It was the look of vulnerability that did it, that was so moving. There was something perfectly extraordinary about looking so gently, incompetently unable to look after himself when he was made of such a large quantity of bone and muscle.

Looking up at him muzzily, Holly said, 'You've grown, Marcus.'

'I know, I don't seem able to stop. Holly—' He swallowed the brandy at a gulp. 'I just wanted to say, I'm awfully sorry, Holly. About Judy. I'm—I'm sorry. That's what I'm trying to say, that I'm sorry. I mean, I don't know how else to put it. It sounds silly to go on saying one's sorry, I know there are better words, but I want you to know how I feel.'

'Leave her in peace,' Andrew said, approaching the fire. He looked almost small, neatly built and very tense beside Marcus. 'She knows you're sorry. Why don't you go and help Isobel with the scrambled eggs?'

'She doesn't like being helped,' Marcus said. 'Holly, I always loved Judy. Ever since I was a child, she was specially good to me. I can't think of anyone who helped me more. When I got mixed up about anything, I could always go to her. Isobel's always thought she'd got answers to everything, but Judy just let one talk. That was what really helped. She always listened. She was always patient. I loved her.'

'I know, Marcus.' Holly had not always been patient with him herself when he had come to her with his problems. He had generally brought them to her first and given her an earnest, agitated account of them, pleading for her interest. But with three years between them, she had been that little amount too old or too young to be kind to him. So he had gone to Judy.

'Of course she knows,' Andrew said. 'Now for God's sake, just go! And don't take another drink with you. You've had enough for this evening.'

It dawned on Holly then that Marcus actually was slightly drunk.

He muttered, 'Don't try to push me around, Andrew.

You keep doing it. It isn't right to push people around. And I wanted Holly to know—because I don't know what people have been telling her about me, and for all I know, she thinks I'm some sort of awful monster—I just want you to know, Holly, I'm desperately sorry about Judy. And I didn't do that thing in the Sea Cave. I know it's not the right time to talk about that, but still, I do want to say, don't listen to anyone who tells you I did. I didn't.'

She did her best to smile up at him through the fog that enshrouded her. 'I'm sure you didn't.'

'Are you?' he said. 'Are you sure?'

The truth was that she was not. Dragged out of her own preoccupations for a moment, she wondered how witnesses who had said that they had seen Marcus in the Sea Cave on the night when the old man had been beaten up could possibly be wrong. How could you be even in doubt whether or not you had seen someone there who was so hugely, colourfully handsome? Marcus would stand out, wherever he was. Of course, someone might be deliberately lying. Marcus with his looks, and his background of wealth, and his innocent-seeming charm, might easily stir up jealousy and malice. Yet Holly found herself recoiling from him. The mere thought of violence, at the moment, made her feel sick. It always had. But she had never felt as scared and outraged by it as she was now. It had never come so close to her before. And if Marcus had really kicked in the ribs of a helpless old man, she did not want to go on looking at him.

Letting her eyes shut, she said, 'Of course I'm sure, Marcus, if you say so.'

'But it's a puzzle why Loraine won't back me up and say I was with her, isn't it?' he said. 'That's all she'd have to do—just say I was with her, because that's all it was. We weren't doing a thing she need mind telling people about. She kept on talking and talking about a new play Lisa's writing and how she was going to be offered a part in it, which I told her obviously wasn't on, but she wouldn't listen—'

'Marcus,' Andrew said, 'go.'

'All right, sorry,' Marcus said. 'But you do understand how I feel about Judy, don't you, Holly? She was trying to help me with Loraine. She was trying to persuade Mrs Gargrave to tell the truth . . . All right, Andrew, I'm going.'

He stooped to give Holly an awkward pat on the shoulder, then took his towering self out of the drawing-room.

After he had gone there was a silence. Holly's eyelids still drooped. They felt almost paralysed. Her head began to nod. Then she felt Andrew sit on the arm of her chair and put an arm round her. It was comforting to let her head rest against his side.

'You don't want to talk about any of it, I suppose,' he said.

'Not much.'

'Could you manage just a little?'

'I expect so. What?'

'Well, do you realize I don't know anything at all? Only that Judy's dead and that it seems to have been murder.'

'Oh, it was murder,' she said. 'You can't commit suicide by hitting yourself over the head with a bronze vase.'

'I wasn't thinking of suicide,' he said. 'Judy wouldn't commit suicide. She was a happy woman. But I was wondering about an accident.'

'Same objection.'

'And if only you hadn't come home, you wouldn't have been caught up in it all.'

'Lucky I did,' Holly said. 'Lucky someone was here. And that reminds me, I ought to send a cable to my father. He's Judy's nearest relative. He and I, we're the only ones. He ought to be told. Could I telephone a cable from here? He's in Sydney.'

'Write what you want to say and I'll do it for you.'

He got up, went to a writing-table and brought her a sheet of paper and a pencil.

'Go on, write,' he said.

'What shall I say?'

'The address first.'

She wrote her father's name and address at the top of the paper, then looked up at Andrew, as if it were for him to dictate her message. She felt quite without initiative.

Andrew accepted the duty she thrust on him.

'Why not say, "Regret to inform you Judy found dead this evening foul play suspected . . ."? No, for God's sake, don't, that's horrible. Say, "Judy found dead in cottage this evening head injuries police investigating." What about that? Is it too bald?'

She wrote it down obediently without questioning it.

'I'll just add, "Will cable further news",' she said. 'I suppose they might fly home, but I don't suppose they will. After all, they can't do anything for her, can they?'

'It's leaving you to carry a pretty heavy load, if they don't,' he said. 'But give it to me, I'll send it.'

She gave him the sheet of paper, but he did not go to the telephone at once. He stood looking down at her.

'Do you know why it happened?' he asked.

'No.'

'Does anyone?'

'Not yet.'

'Was it simple robbery?'

'I don't think the police think so,' she answered. 'They seem to believe it was someone Judy knew. You see, soon after I left the cottage, someone came to it and had a drink with her. They had it out on the terrace. That means it must have been soon after I left, because they wouldn't have had it outside if it had started to rain. And Judy drank sherry and whoever was with her drank beer. Then it's as if he attacked her out there. The table and two chairs were overturned and the glasses were broken.

And Judy ran inside and he followed her and snatched up the vase and beat her with it. I think that's how the police think it happened.'

'Don't you?'

'Oh, they're right about all that, I expect,' she said. 'They know about that sort of thing. But I feel so muddled and stupid, I can't think. If it was someone she knew there'd have to be a *why*, and I simply can't think of one. Who could there be to whom Judy would give a drink who'd then set about cold-bloodedly murdering her?'

'As you've described it, it sounds more hot-blooded than cold.'

'Well, whichever it was, can you think of anyone around here who's been getting odd lately, doing peculiar things, getting talked about?'

Andrew gave her a curious look, as if he were trying to read something in her expression, but she was too tired to think about it at the time. It was only later that it occurred to her that he had, of course, thought that she was hinting at Marcus.

After a moment, he said, 'I wish I'd gone into the cottage with you. I only thought of it after I'd driven away and realized there was something odd about the whole place being in darkness.'

'I wasn't alone long,' she said. 'Lisa Chard and Stephen Floyd turned up and they stayed till Ben and I left. What's wrong with those two, Andrew? They seemed to be trying to help me, yet they couldn't stop needling one another all the time.'

'I think he's in love with her and she isn't with him, that's all,' Andrew said.

'Is Lisa in love with Ben?' She was thinking of the subtle change that had come over Lisa as soon as Ben had come into the room, the way that she had preened herself before him.

Andrew gave Holly a startled look. Yet he did not seem truly surprised, and it occurred to her that he had the same thought in his mind and that this, and not Marcus, was the trouble of which he had spoken earlier.

His answer was short, however. 'I've only met her a couple of times. I hardly know her. Look, here's your soup.'

It was Kate who brought it in, in a blue and white Copenhagen soup bowl on a tray, which she arranged on Holly's knees.

'The scrambled eggs and the coffee will be along in a minute or two,' Kate said. 'The soup's marvellous—one of mother's specials that she can't ever repeat, because it's got a bit of everything in it. It began with the bones of the duck we had a few days ago, then there were some vegetables and gravy over from a veal casserole, then there were other odds and ends, mushrooms and tomatoes and so on. Try it—it'll make you feel a lot better.'

Holly did, and found it was just as delicious as Kate had said, and its warmth and richness, sliding down into her, made her feel far better than the brandy that she had had earlier.

'Ben's eating in the kitchen,' Kate went on, 'and looks as if he's in the sort of mood in which one doesn't interrupt him. I don't know why he is, because, d'you know, to be absolutely honest, he never liked Judy much. He put up with her because she was such a close friend of Isobel's, but he always said she was a chattering old hen who'd get done in some day for talking too much.'

'Kate, don't!' Andrew said sharply.

'Sorry,' Kate said. 'Of course he didn't mean that literally. And I don't suppose it actually happened because she talked out of turn, do you? After all, who cares nowadays what's said about them? You can accuse people of absolutely anything, and nobody's going to murder you for it.'

She drifted out of the room again. Andrew also went out to telephone Holly's cable to Sydney. As he went, Isobel came in with the scrambled eggs and the coffee. She sat watching Holly eat, but her eyes were so preoccupied that Holly doubted if she saw her. Isobel seemed quite lost in her thoughts, and whatever thoughts they were, Holly was glad, from the look on her face, that they were not hers. She did not see Ben again that evening. She only heard him presently, speaking in a loud, angry voice in the kitchen, when Kate was taking her up to her room. The next moment the kitchen door slammed and Marcus came out into the hall. His normally fresh pink cheeks had big blotches of angry red on them.

'D'you know what he's been saying to me?' he shouted up at Kate and Holly as they stood on the stairs. 'He's been asking me if I went to Cross Cottage this evening and had a drink with Judy. I said I didn't, and he said, "I don't believe you." I said again I didn't, and he said, "You told us all you were going there." '

'So you did,' Kate said. 'I remember now, you told us so at lunch. You said you were going to ask Judy if she'd got anywhere with Mrs Gargrave.'

'But I didn't go!'

'Sure?'

He scowled at her. 'What d'you take me for? Of course I'm sure.'

'Then that's all right, isn't it?' Kate said blandly, and led the way on up the stairs to the room that had been got ready for Holly. 'What a pity Marcus is such a liar,' she said. 'I bet he went. Now are you going to be all right, Holly? I mean, alone in here? You won't have nightmares? If it's going to worry you, I could move in with you for the night.'

This was unusually considerate of Kate, who was not accustomed to thinking about how other people felt. But Holly answered, 'No, thanks very much, I'll be quite all right.'

'What about taking one of those pills Isobel was talking about?' Kate suggested.

'I don't think anything would keep me awake.'

'I'll be in the same old room at the end of the passage,

if you find you do want one, or anything else,' Kate said. 'I'll probably be grateful if you wake me. I foresee a night of bad dreams.'

She went out.

When Holly got into bed and turned out the light, she thought that all that she would have to do to let sleep engulf her and blot out the horror of the evening, was to lie down and close her eyes. It was an illusion. In fact what happened, as soon as the room was dark, was that she found herself back in the aeroplane in which she had started that day's journeyings. Only she was having a far rougher trip than she had had that morning. Every time that sleep seemed near, the aircraft dipped sickeningly under her, while the noise of the engines hummed like thunder in her ears.

She kept thinking of the wilting roses and the empty vase beside the sink in the cottage, of the overturned table and chairs and the broken glasses on the terrace. When at last she fell asleep, she had a dream, which would have been a nightmare if there had been any terror in it, but the mood of it was only of depression and an odd sense of guilt.

She dreamt that Andrew was in the big drawing-room, walking towards the round bay at the end, and that three reflections of him in the three tall windows came to meet him out of the dark garden. Yet it turned out, when they were near enough to be seen clearly, that none of them was of him. They were all of Holly, and as soon as he saw her, he gave a start and turned and walked away from the window. And as he did so, her three reflections were compelled to turn away too and disappear. She wanted desperately to stay, but it was impossible. As long as he kept his back turned and went on walking away, she had to keep her back turned too and go on walking.

It was Andrew who woke her next morning, bringing her breakfast on a tray. He looked as if he had not slept any more than she had. But he managed a smile of sorts.

'Wonderful service you get in this house, don't you?' he said. 'I have to report, however, that the toast's burnt, the milk's boiled over, the coffee's lousy, and it's all my doing. But you seemed in danger of being altogether forgotten by everyone else, so I thought I'd better try my hand at getting you something. But I'm afraid my mind wasn't on my work, and I've forgotten the marmalade. Shall I go and get it, or can you live without it?'

Holly sat up in bed.

'What's been happening?' she asked, yawning expansively.

He planted the tray on her lap.

'The police are here,' he said. 'They've been here for the last hour. And ever so politely they've asked Marcus to go back into Helsington with them.'

'Marcus? They've arrested him?' She almost upset the tray all over the bed.

'Not arrested him,' Andrew said. 'Not charged him. They just want him to help them with their inquiries.'

## CHAPTER V

'WHY MARCUS?' Holly asked.

'Because when they came here they told us there were fingerprints on the beer bottle found on Judy's terrace,' Andrew said. 'It was sheltered from the rain by one of the chairs, so the fingerprints hadn't got washed off. And when Marcus heard that, he simply broke down and said he knew they'd find out the prints were his and that he'd had a drink with Judy on the terrace yesterday evening.'

'Then why did he say last night he hadn't?'

'He says he was scared. He scares very easily. And lying comes naturally to him. When he was younger we used to call it a vivid imagination, do you remember?'

'Then they'll charge him, won't they?' Holly said. 'It's almost a confession.'

'Not quite,' said Andrew. 'He's admitted he was there. He's admitted he and Judy had drinks together. But he denies upsetting the table and breaking the glasses, and he denies harming Judy. Just so much sense of self-preservation he seems to have. For which let us be thankful.'

'You believe him, do you?'

'He's my brother, I want to believe him.'

Holly nodded. 'I want the murderer to be someone I never heard of before and needn't ever see.'

'You'll probably have to see him when it comes to the trial.'

'Then I hope he has a face which won't mean anything to me.'

'If you should actually feel inclined to try to help Marcus . . .' Andrew paused, looking down at her. 'Do you want to help?'

'Just how can I?' she asked.

'I thought it might be interesting to talk to Loraine Gargrave.'

'That might not help at all.'

'I know, it might do the opposite. But I thought it might be interesting to find out what sort of girl she is. Marcus says he went to the Gargraves after he left Judy and took Loraine out for a drink in the Plough and Sickle to try to persuade her to tell the truth about what happened in the Sea Cave. And that at least can be checked. He's known in the Plough and Sickle and if he was there with Loraine, the fact will have been noted, whatever she says. And I'd rather like to hear her side of the Sea Cave story for myself.'

'All right,' Holly said, 'as soon as I'm up.'

He went out, leaving her to her breakfast.

It was almost as bad as he had said. The toast had been singed, the milk smelled faintly burned and the coffee was the instant kind, made staggeringly strong, so that all it tasted of was unadulterated bitterness. Andrew was not domesticated, that was evident. All the same, Holly ate and drank enough to feel that she could face the day ahead, then got out of bed and had a bath, and about half an hour later, dressed in slacks and a sweater, went downstairs.

She found a quarrel in progress between Ben and Isobel. She had heard enough of these in the past not to be alarmed. They flared up suddenly, and died down as rapidly. At the time Ben generally appeared to be the winner, because he would raise his voice and shout down anything that Isobel had to say, but afterwards Isobel generally did as she had intended all along. Though she seemed to be unaware of it herself, always seeing herself as accommodating her behaviour to other people's, she had an extremely strong will, and was very seldom to be deflected from anything which she had set her heart on doing.

They were in the dining-room, facing one another across the table, with the remains of breakfast between them. The room was in the oldest part of the house and had a low, heavily beamed ceiling and two small windows with leaded panes. The furniture, of course, had all been made by Ben, and was of yew tree, which looked pleasantly light, without seeming out of place, in the ancient room.

'You choose today of all days,' Ben was shouting, 'to try this margarine kick again! Haven't I told you I won't eat the stuff? I personally ate all the margarine I ever intend to for the rest of my life during the war and I consider we earned the right then to decent butter now. What I want is decent butter. We aren't paupers.'

'Not paupers,' Isobel agreed. 'We're very fortunate people in many ways. In this present crisis we at least needn't worry overmuch about our financial position. We can see Marcus gets the best legal aid, if he needs it. Think what it would be like now if we were poor. But I still think that a few reasonable economies never come amiss.'

'That's sheer miserliness, that's what it is!' Ben bellowed. 'You're a very rich woman, Isobel, but you behave like a miser.'

She took it calmly. 'I shouldn't have thought you were the person to hurl that accusation at me just at the moment, Ben,' she said. 'When you asked me for money for those new tools you want, I didn't refuse, did I?'

He drew his breath in and made an obvious effort to control himself.

'No, you didn't—I'm sorry, Isobel. Forget what I said, if you can.'

'I'm not generally stingy about anything important, am I?' she said. 'But one of us has to think about money sometimes.'

'Yes, yes,' he said. 'Of course. But no more margarine!'

'All right, I'll finish it up in the cooking—' Isobel broke off as she became aware of Holly standing in the doorway. 'Holly, you've had no breakfast! What selfish beasts we are! But we've had the police here, questioning us all about our movements yesterday evening, because they seem to have absolutely made up their minds that Judy was killed by someone she knew, and they've taken Marcus away with them to the police station, all because he admitted he dropped in on Judy yesterday evening and had a drink with her. But he didn't upset the table and chairs, or break the glasses, and of course he didn't do poor Judy any harm whatever. He says he left Judy about seven, then went to see that horrible little Loraine Gargrave, the stupid boy, as if she hasn't done enough harm already, and then he came home. That was about eight o'clock, quite soon after you left. So you see, he couldn't have done anything to Judy. Now what would you like for breakfast? You didn't have much to eat last night, so you ought to have something solid.'

'I've had breakfast, thank you,' Holly said. 'Andrew brought it up to me.'

'Andrew? Oh no!' Isobel's tone was one of startled

protest. 'That's quite unlike him. He never lifts a finger to help in the house. Oh, why is everyone being so unlike themselves? It's the last straw. And here are Ben and I, wasting our time arguing about whether or not you can tell margarine from butter, which I don't believe for a moment you can—'

'*I* can!' Ben growled.

'Well, anyway, we're wasting our time,' she rattled on, 'when we ought to be getting a lawyer for poor Marcus. Ben, do ring up Inglis and Inglis straight away. Do please do it now! Oh God, why do I have to think of everything all the time? No one else in the house seems to have any practical sense at all . . . No, don't bother, Ben, I'll do it. But can you be ready to drive into Helsington straight away if I can get an appointment with one of the Inglis brothers this morning?'

He grunted an answer, nodding.

Isobel shot past Holly out of the room and a moment later was talking rapidly into the telephone.

Ben strolled to one of the windows and stood with his back to the room, looking out.

'I'm sorry to have let you in on that stupid little scene, Holly,' he said. 'All my fault. I'm rattled, so I take it out on Isobel. I always do. But it doesn't mean anything. Isobel's done everything for me always. Given me my home, looked after my family, seen that I had peace to get on with my work. Given me my work itself, you might say, because I could never have made a living at it. It's a hopelessly uneconomic occupation in these days of the triumph of the second-rate. Without her, I'd have had to compromise. I'd have to do cheap, shoddy work, or even give up altogether and do something else. And she's quite right, at a time like this, I'm nothing. I leave everything to her, just as I do at other times. I'm not sure, as a matter of fact, that that isn't part of the cause of what's been happening to Marcus. To Kate too, if it comes to that. They've both got the idea that life consists of just comfortably depending on their mother. They're a useless pair. They ought to have been made to go out and earn their livings at some ordinary kind of job that wasn't beyond their capacities—because neither of them has any special talent, though Isobel can't see that. They'd be happier in the end, doing that, than going on looking for some vague thing that was going to fulfil their personalities to perfection.'

His voice had dropped to a mutter. Holly had begun to wonder if he had forgotten that she was there and was just talking to himself.

He went on, 'Andrew's different, of course. He always has been. He's always known exactly where he was going. In that way he's more like me than any of the others. He's got more of me in him than either of them. Perhaps that's why we don't get on with each other particularly well. It's at least one of the reasons he had to go and live abroad. He had to make the break with us all as complete as possible.'

From behind Holly, Andrew said, 'I've got the car out. Are you ready to go, Holly?'

She was glad to go. The two village women who did the housework for Isobel had arrived, and the house reverberated to the domestic sounds of vacuum-cleaner and dishwasher, of plodding feet and chattering voices. The voices were full of hushed excitement. Both Miss Gill and Mrs Willand were sure that it was them hooligans from Helsington as done it and that the police couldn't be counted on to raise a finger, because they were scared of them, right down scared. It was different when it came to parking offences or dropping litter, then they were down on you fast enough, but with a thing like this they never got anywhere. When the two women saw Holly, their faces developed a predatory look, a look she knew, and thought of as the coffee look. It meant that soon she would have coffee and biscuits thrust upon her, and would be expected to offer a fair exchange in the form of information and drama.

She and Andrew went out to the car.

The Gargraves' cottage was in the main street of Roydon Saint Agnes, next to the Plough and Sickle, which was one of the four pubs in the village, a characterless red-brick building, very neat and clean, which advertised coffee and sandwiches and snacks as well as beer and spirits. Opposite to it was the village hall, which, as usual, was plastered with notices of all the social events in the village, coming or long past, whist drives, activities connected with the Harvest Festival, a lecture on the pre-history of the neighbourhood, an old people's outing. The sight stabbed Holly with grief. If Judy had been alive, she would have been involved in everything. Next to the hall was the post office, in which you could buy everything from aspirins to shoe-laces, and a few doors farther on the shop kept by Mrs Gargrave's sister, which was in an old cottage that had recently had a brand new shop-front built on to it. The rest of the street consisted mainly of small houses, lived in by elderly retired civil servants, professors, colonels, and a few farm labourers, who were lucky enough to have leases that could not be broken.

The Gargraves' cottage was white and very old with a roof of decayed-looking thatch and windows so small that they suggested a dungeon-like darkness inside. There was a small strip of garden in front in which a few autumn flowers toppled forlornly amongst weeds. Obviously no one in the household was an enthusiastic gardener. Since the household consisted of Mrs Gargrave, her father and Loraine, this was not surprising. For Mrs Gargrave was sixty-three, had varicose veins and Judy's house to look after as well as her own, and did odd afternoons besides for other ladies. Her father was eighty-seven, and although he had once been the most active of odd-job men in the village, nowadays could only just manage to walk to the Plough and Sickle and back. And Loraine had her career to consider. So naturally the michaelmas daisies, stubborn as they were, were being beaten by the willowherb and nettles.

Mrs Gargrave came to the door when Andrew knocked. She was a small, broadly-built woman, wide at the shoulders, wide at the hips, with the space between filled in with rolls of soft, bouncing flesh. Her face was square, wholesome and good-natured. She had plump calves, but neat ankles and small feet. She was wearing pink bedroom-slippers, no stockings and a much-washed cotton dress, with a black and white checked apron over it, embroidered with a pattern of kittens, appliquéd in pink felt.

Her jaw dropped and her pleasant blue eyes grew sombre as soon as she saw Holly and Andrew.

'Oh, it's you, Miss Holly,' she said. 'Good morning, Mr Andrew. This is a dreadful thing. I'm glad you're here though, Miss Holly. I didn't know you was coming. She said nothing about it. The last time I saw her she and me had the one and only quarrel we ever had in all the years I been working for her. I don't mean we didn't have our disagreements. We did and they always ended up with Miss Dunthorne saying, "Well, we'll agree to differ, shall we, Mrs Gargrave?" And I'd say, "Well, we've all got a right to our opinions, haven't we, Miss Dunthorne?" And she'd say, "Yes, it's a free country, Mrs Gargrave." And that'd be that. But this other time was different. She really hurt my feelings, Miss Holly. And then my veins got bad, so we never had the chance to make it up. If you'd care to come in for a cup of coffee now . . .?'

Holly knew that there would be no escaping the coffee if they wanted to talk to her.

'Thank you, if you aren't too busy.'

'Oh, I'm not specially busy.' Mrs Gargrave turned and led the way to the sitting-room. 'I'm not doing more than I can help, because of my veins. I'm saving my legs all I can. And He's sitting out at the back.' She was speaking of her aged father. 'He likes to sit out in the sun as long as it's warm enough. Poor old soul, it's one of the only pleasures he has left. I'm sure I hope I don't live to his age, specially seeing I haven't anyone to look after me, like he's got me.'

'I thought you'd a son, Mrs Gargrave,' Andrew said. 'And there's your granddaughter for whom you've done so much.'

They had entered the minute sitting-room, which was crammed with furniture, little tables, plant-stands, whatnots and chairs of all shapes and sizes, because Mrs Gargrave had always been totally unable to say no to a gift. As a result the cast-off possessions of all the ladies for whom she had ever worked, all the worn-out or useless things to which they had taken a sudden dislike and which, without Mrs Gargrave, would have found their way to jumble sales or on to bonfires, had accumulated in her tiny room until there was barely space for normal life to go on there.

'Just make yourselves comfortable,' she said as Andrew and Holly threaded their way between these objects, to chairs. Holly's chair was one she recognized as having come from Judy's house. Its cover had once been a deep, warm red, but had faded patchily to a sickly shrimp colour. 'And please smoke if you want to, but I can't offer cigarettes, as Loraine is the only one smokes in this house, since He gave it up because of his bronchitis, and she always takes hers along with her.'

'Then she isn't in,' Holly said.

'No, she's at the theatre, rehearsing,' Mrs Gargrave said importantly. 'You know about her and the theatre, do you, Miss Holly? She's always rehearsing. She works terribly hard. Comes home sometimes in the evenings ready to drop. But she hasn't got another thought in her head. She's dedicated, that's what it is.'

'How did it start?' Holly asked.

'It all started with my veins last Christmas,' Mrs Gargrave said. 'I'd been going to Miss Chard Tuesday and Friday afternoons for a few weeks—she hadn't been here long—and what with me only just having started working for her, I didn't like to let her down, and over Christmas too, when she'd got guests coming, but the pain was terrible, so Loraine went along, just to help me out. Of course Loraine has always been mad about anything to do with acting—she used always to have the best part in the school play, only you wouldn't remember that, I suppose—so when she heard Miss Chard wrote plays and had them filmed and on television and everything, she was really quite excited about going to work for her. Then she got Miss Chard to go and see her act in a play they did in the village hall, and Miss Chard said she really had talent and ought to do something about it. Now I'll get the coffee. I shan't be a moment.'

She bustled out.

'Clever Loraine,' Andrew murmured, when she had gone. 'There's nothing like seizing a chance, is there? Or manufacturing one.'

'I suppose it *was* manufactured, her going to work for Lisa,' said Holly.

'What else?'

They sat in silence till Mrs Gargrave returned with three cups of very milky coffee and a plate of sweet biscuits.

When she had handed them round she sat down and smoothed her apron over her knees with a gesture that looked as if she were stroking the pink felt kittens.

'You came to talk about Loraine, didn't you?' she said. 'About her and Mr Marcus.'

'Yes,' Andrew said and nibbled a biscuit. 'To see if you can't help him.'

'I'd talk if it was any help to him,' she said. 'I'd be glad to. He's a good boy, or he was till he took up with those roughs in Helsington. What his parents are doing, allowing it, I can't imagine. They aren't his class at all. And he's too good-natured and too sort of innocent, if you understand me, to see what he's getting into till it's too late. Then too, he can't stand drink. Loraine's often said so. She says he ought to keep off it till he can control himself better. It was drink was his trouble in the Sea

Cave. I doubt if he even knew what he was doing to the poor old fellow they seen him kicking. Well, it's a nasty story, and I'm sorry for his poor parents, and I'm sorry for Mr Marcus too, who, as I was saying, was a nice boy once, and I hope he'll grow out of this sort of thing while he still can. But I don't think he should have tried to drag our Loraine in the mud just to help himself. She's a working girl and she's got her way to make in the world. It isn't like for him. His parents can afford to pay his fine and they can send him away to a university or something till it's all forgotten.'

'Mrs Gargrave, it may not be a fine this time,' Andrew said. 'It may be prison.'

Her hand, stroking the pink kittens on her apron, was still for a moment, then moved faster, as if she were having trouble keeping them in order.

'He shouldn't have tried to drag our Loraine in the mud,' she repeated.

'I don't see anything very muddy about admitting she went for a drive with Marcus,' Andrew said.

'Only it isn't true! She was here at home with me. Can you prove anything else? Has anyone else come forward to say they saw her in the Sea Cave?'

That was the trouble, of course. Nobody had.

'All the same, I believe she and my brother went for that drive,' Andrew said.

Mrs Gargrave gave him a sad smile in which there was genuine sympathy.

'I know how you feel, Mr Andrew,' she said. 'I would too, if he was my brother. I'm sorry for him as it is. And if Loraine could help him, I'd say . . . Well, I'm not sure what I'd say, that's the truth. I'll tell you something that taught me a lesson once. It was with my Bob. That's Loraine's father. He lives in Liverpool and he's doing well at last, thank God. His second wife steadied him up. She's hard, she hasn't got much heart, but she's been good for him. I was just too soft, and Linda—that was his first wife—was no good to anyone. Well, what happened was this. Bob was only nineteen at the time. Him and some young fellows he was going around with was in a pub in Helsington when someone give one of the fellows a shove. A shove in the back with an elbow. And he turned and said, "Who done that?" That's all. "Who done that?" he said. Maybe he said it loud like, but Bob saw it all and he said that's all the fellow done. But the bouncer in the pub threw him out, and he was charged with assault, and there were people there ready to swear they'd seen him hit the other fellow. Because he'd been up in court once before, you see, that's the way it was. But Bob said to his father, who was alive then, "Dad," he said, "I'm going into court to say he never done nothing. He's innocent," Bob said, "and I'm going into court to say so." '

As she grew absorbed in her story, Mrs Gargrave's hands folded loosely in her lap, leaving the kittens in peace.

She went on, 'But Mr Gargrave said, "You aren't going into no court, my lad. You've got a job now and your mother and me can't afford to let you lose a day's pay." And Bob said, "But he's innocent, Dad!" And Mr Gargrave said, "A son of mine isn't going into no court to have mud thrown at him. Mud sticks, lad," he said. So Bob give in. Then the fellow's mother come to me and said, "Mrs Gargrave," she said, "my boy's innocent. All he ever done was turn on this fellow who give him the shove and call out, 'Who done that?' And your boy knows that, so won't he go into court and clear my boy's name for him?" Well, I could feel for her, but remembering what Mr Gargrave said, I said how we couldn't afford for Bob to lose a day's pay not going to work. Times were hard with us then, with Mr Gargrave off sick going on for six months. He never got well, poor chap. He went that winter.'

She lifted her coffee cup and sipped it thoughtfully. She wasn't looking at either Andrew or Holly, but apparently at some bulrushes in a china umbrella-stand that stood by the fireplace. Really her gaze went inward, to something that had happened a long time ago.

'So this fellow's mother says to me, "We'll make up Bob's pay for him if he'll go and speak up for my boy." I said that made it different, but still I wasn't sure what Mr Gargrave would say, but I said I'd tell him and see. But he still said no, Bob wasn't going into court to get himself a bad name. But Bob went all the same. We couldn't stop him. "The chap's innocent," he said, "so I've got to go." And he went. Not that it made any difference. They wouldn't listen to a boy like Bob. The other fellow was found guilty and fined five pound. And then—and *then*—' Mrs Gargrave sat up very straight in her chair and looked Andrew straight in the face. 'Then, Mr Andrew, someone here in Roydon says to me next day, "I was in court yesterday because of that parking without lights trouble my Derek had and I see your Bob there. How much did they fine him?" I drew myself up haughty and I said, "Listen," I said, "they didn't fine him nothing. He wasn't charged with nothing, not even parking without lights. He was a witness. He went there to clear the name of his friend. He was only doing his duty." But then one person after another kept on asking me how much Bob been fined, and that was when he began to get a name for being wild, and he started going more and more with a wild lot, till he got that girl Linda into trouble and had to marry her. And Linda was never any good and they were never happy together like Mr Gargrave and me, and Bob never really settled down till she left him and he married Theresa and went to this job of his in Liverpool. So that's why I won't have Loraine going into court.'

'Even though she *was* with him, wasn't she, Mrs Gargrave?' Andrew said gently.

She gave one of the pink kittens, which happened to be stretched tight over one of her plump knees, a hard slap.

'Listen, Mr Andrew,' she said, 'I said to her, "I learnt a

lesson with your father I won't never forget. If he'd taken notice of his dad, his whole life would've been different. So don't think you're going into court even to help Mr Marcus." She's ever so good-natured, you see, Loraine is. She'd do anything to help a friend. But I'm not having her standing up there in public and getting mud thrown at her for anyone.'

Andrew and Holly exchanged glances. Holly did not think that they were going to get any farther here. Mrs Gargrave might be the sort of woman who was slow to learn a lesson, but what she had learnt, she had learnt for life. But Andrew was not yet ready to leave the matter there.

'Forgetting what happened at the Sea Cave,' he said, 'what about last night? Did Marcus come here and did he and Loraine go out for a drink together?'

Mrs Gargrave thought deeply before she answered, trying to decide if there were any traps in the question, trying to find the safest way to tread. After a moment she decided. 'Yes, he did,' she said. 'He come here it might be seven o'clock, quarter past, and said he wanted to talk to Loraine. And she said she didn't want to talk to him, she wanted to wash her hair, but he said, "Oh, come along," so she went with him and they went to the Plough, then he brought her back and went off home. Well, I suppose it was home he went. Loraine wasn't gone more than half an hour.'

That fitted with what Marcus himself had told the police. Andrew and Holly exchanged glances again, agreeing that this time it was time to go. They thanked Mrs Gargrave for her coffee, then wended their way out through the little tables and the plant-stands to the door.

As they went to the car, Holly said, 'Where now?'

'I thought the theatre,' he answered.

'You think it'll be any use talking to Loraine, after what we've listened to?'

He started the car. 'I still want to see what sort of girl she is.'

Driving through the village to the crossroads, they passed Cross Cottage, which had a police car standing in front of it, then they passed the collection of white cubes that was Lisa Chard's house, then went on towards Helsington. The morning was clear and bright. The fields of stubble on either side of the road shone in softly changing tones of gold. It would have been a wonderful day for the drive and the picnic that Holly and Andrew had planned the day before.

'That was a moral story we listened to just now,' Holly observed.

'With a very complicated moral,' Andrew agreed.

'It was one way of saying that there's one law for the rich and another for the poor.'

'Yes, according to Mrs Gargrave's view, going into court was the beginning of her son's slide downhill, so it's right for her to try to protect Loraine from the same sort of disaster. A little matter like perverting justice wouldn't enter into it. Justice is mainly something that gets used against you, if you aren't very wary.'

'And I'd swear still she's an utterly honest person.'

'Oh, she is, she is,' he said. 'That's where the moral comes in. She'd lie to the end to protect you, if you needed it, just so long as it didn't conflict with a deeper loyalty, like this one to Loraine. Isn't that being as honest as most of us manage to be?'

Holly looked at his profile, noticing how his features had tightened up since the day before.

'You're awfully worried about Marcus, aren't you?' she said.

'Wouldn't you be?'

'But Mrs Gargrave almost said she didn't think he'd done that thing in the Sea Cave. And you can't really be afraid he's turned into the sort of monster he'd have to be to have killed Judy.'

'He used that word himself last night, didn't he?—monster,' Andrew said. 'And you know, I think, in our family, we're all of us monsters of some kind. We're all exaggerations of something or other. Something in each of us has got over-size and out of proportion. Ben's exaggeratedly dedicated to his non-commercial art, Isobel to the welfare of the family, Kate to desperation and boredom and drink—increasingly drink. Marcus too, and he can't carry it as Kate can. It rather frightens me when I see how sober that girl stays when I know just how much she's sunk.'

'You haven't said what sort of monster you are,' Holly said.

'I think I'm probably over-absorbed in my job and abnormally careful to avoid entanglements. Mainly with my family, but with other people too. Holding off from my family has given me the habit of holding off from everybody . . .' His voice faltered. 'It's made me do some very stupid things.'

'Yet it's so obvious you're fond of them all,' Holly said. 'You may not be aware of it, but you are.'

'Oh yes, I'm fond of them,' he replied. 'Even of Marcus, though I haven't succeeded in having one sensible talk with him since I've been home. But I'm fond of the damned boy, I can't help it, and I'm just as worried about him as you say. So is everyone else, of course, that's an effect he has on people. And that may have been his ruination.'

'Do you know, when I was a child,' Holly said, 'I used to think it would be the most wonderful thing in the world to belong to your family. You were all so free, going to that school where you didn't have to wear uniform or do any work if you didn't want to, and calling your parents by their first names, and having that huge old house and all this lovely country to roam in, and just being yourselves without any interference from anybody. I wanted so much to belong to you, I used literally to pray for it.'

'That's a prayer that could be answered more easily now than then,' Andrew said. 'Marry me.' But before Holly could even turn her head again to look at him in her astonishment, he went straight on, 'Only there's a right time and a wrong time for saying a thing, isn't there? And this is the wrong time. The truth is, we're strangers. We only met for the first time yesterday. Now we've got to find the Market Theatre.'

## CHAPTER VI

THE MARKET THEATRE was in what had once been a warehouse near to the Covered Market of Helsington. The Covered Market was a warren of butchers' shops, fishmongers, greengrocers, health food stores, stalls where cheap printed cottons were sold, and pet shops where you could buy anything from what was nominally an Alsatian puppy to a budgerigar. Andrew parked the car in the car-park nearest to the market, then he and Holly wandered up and down the colourful alleys until they found an arrow directing them to the theatre.

It was a theatre club as well as a theatre. Most of the ground floor was occupied by a bar and a restaurant of sorts. A strong smell of packet soups and tinned spaghetti hung about it. In the bar some local artist was having his work exhibited. The paint was thick and crusty and he used an amazing amount of dark red, which gave his pictures the rather gruesome appearance of having been splashed with blood that had dried there. The bar was moderately full of young men and women, most of them dressed in jeans and jerseys, and all economically drinking beer or soft drinks. The restaurant, however, was full of fast-eating, middle-aged men and women who looked as if they worked in the market. A good many of them wore overalls, some of them blood-stained from their work in the butchers' shops, and some decorated with glittering, sequin-like herring scales. They looked the sort of people who would sit evening after evening in front of the television, rather than be seen dead in this theatre, but who had discovered that, after paying a small subscription, it was a convenient place to eat.

No one asked Holly and Andrew if they were members or questioned their right to be there. Andrew went up to the bar and spoke to the bearded young man behind it.

'I'm looking for Miss Gargrave,' he said. 'Loraine Gargrave.'

The young man nodded towards a door at the end of the bar.

'Through there,' he said. 'I saw her come in. Are you press?'

'No,' Andrew said.

'Oh, I thought you must be,' the young man said. 'The police were here a little while ago, talking to her, and in this town the press follows the police as the night the day. No one else supplies any news. Pity you aren't press. She'd have liked that.'

They went through the door, and found nothing there but a small, chilly lobby, pervaded by a faint smell of mildew, with a stone staircase, leading down into a basement. Voices came from below. Holly and Andrew went down and through an open door and found themselves in the theatre.

It was the kind of theatre that has its stage in the middle, with seats all round it. The seats might have held a hundred people, while the stage was about twenty foot square, with a cone over the top of it from which light fell on a group of people. They were discussing the sandwiches that each wanted for lunch while a young girl in black jeans and a black jersey, with glossy black hair hanging over her shoulders, and long copper ear-rings, was trying to memorize their orders.

'Danish salami for John,' she said, 'and liver sausage for Maurice, and cheese for Wendy, and what was it for Eric? —oh, that was cheese too—and ham for Lynne, and pickled onions for John and Maurice and gherkins for Eric . . .

Danish salami for John, and liver sausage for Maurice . . .' As if it were a part in a play that she was trying to learn, she repeated it as she came towards the door and found herself face to face with Andrew and Holly.

She stopped with a startled intake of breath and her eyes went swiftly from one to the other. They were very expressive eyes, large and dark under low, straight brows, with very long, curving lashes.

'I know you,' she said. 'You're Marcus's brother. And you're that niece of Miss Dunthorne's.'

She was of medium height and very slender. If she was really as much as seventeen it was astonishing, for she looked as if she were only just growing into her adolescence, a lovely, insubstantial waif of thirteen or fourteen.

'You're Loraine Gargrave, aren't you?' Andrew said.

'What do you want?' The beautiful dark eyes, seen close, did not match the rest of her. They did not look at all adolescent or immature.

'A talk,' Andrew said.

'About Marcus?'

'Mainly, of course. We've just had a talk with your grandmother.'

'Then you'll know I've nothing to say.' Her voice was warm and sweet, even when she was keeping it carefully expressionless. She would have to do a little work on her accent, but the sheer richness and clarity that apparently came naturally to her might carry her far.

'That's just what I don't feel certain of,' Andrew said.

'Why not?'

'It's hard to believe you always let her speak for you.'

'But can't you see I'm busy? Please go away.' Frowning, she began to count on her fingers and mutter, 'Danish salami for John, liver sausage for Maurice . . .'

'We came to ask you if you'd have lunch with us,' Andrew said. 'Not here. We want to be able to talk privately. Say at the Crown.'

'I can't,' she said. 'We're just having a break now, but

we'll be working all the afternoon. And if it's about Marcus, I've told the police everything I know, and Mrs Meriden too.'

'My mother—you've seen her this morning?' Andrew said in surprise.

'No, that was some time ago, about the Sea Cave.'

'But you saw the police today.'

'Just for a few minutes.' Her dark glance was steady on Andrew's face. Holly might not have been there. She began to think it was a pity that she had come, for you could see that Loraine was a girl who would always talk more readily to a man than to a woman.

'I wish you'd come with us,' Andrew said in his gentle, almost affectionate way, with his steady eyes appraisingly on her face.

Temptation showed on it. Lunch at the Crown seemed to appeal to her a good deal more than liver sausage or salami. She said uncertainly, 'I'd kind of like to have a talk with you. There are some things that are sort of complicated, that I somehow can't think out by myself. I haven't been feeling good about any of it, that's the truth. But I haven't known what to do.'

'Then it might help if you talked to us.'

'It might make it worse,' she said. 'Talking often does.'

'Not if you only talked to Miss Dunthorne and me,' said Andrew.

'But I'm so busy.' From her tone, it was clear that she did not need much more persuading.

'Why don't you go and ask those people if they can spare you for a little while?' he suggested. 'We needn't be gone long.'

'Well—all right, I'll see what they say.' She went back to talk to John, Maurice, Wendy and the others.

They were in the midst of a discussion of whether a character in the play that they were rehearsing should be portrayed as a truly tender woman or a secretly aggressive one. If any of them was capable of conveying the difference, since it was hard enough to guess at in real life, Holly thought, she might have quite a future ahead of her. They made no difficulties about letting Loraine go. A free lunch, they seemed to think, was something that no one could be reasonably expected to refuse. Loraine picked up an old green anorak from a chair and rejoined Holly and Andrew.

The Crown, which was in the main street of Helsington, had once been a coaching inn and had gables and leaded windows and a slight tilt forward over the street. It had a restaurant, a snack-bar and a lounge bar. The lounge bar, into which they went, had a great many horse brasses and coaching prints on the walls, and a vast fireplace, in the heart of which the artificial logs of an electric fire flickered rhythmically. There was a bowl of yellow plastic chrysanthemums on the bar.

The three of them sat down at one of the little round tables. But if Andrew had planned to use strong drink to make Loraine talk, she foiled him at once by asking for a tonic with just some ice and a slice of lemon in it. No, thank you, she said, no gin. Definitely no gin. She very seldom drank anything, and never at midday. It made her feel queer for the rest of the day. When the tonic came, she sipped it warily, almost as if she suspected gin might have been smuggled into it.

'Well,' she said, 'what do you want to know?'

'I thought we might begin with yesterday evening,' Andrew said. 'You know they took Marcus off to the police station this morning, don't you? For all I know, they've charged him already.'

'With murdering Miss Dunthorne?' She lowered her eyes, gazing hard at her tonic. 'Yes, they told me they'd taken him along. They're crazy.'

'Are they?'

She looked up at him quickly. 'Don't you think so?'

'I do, but why should you?'

'What time do they think he did it?'

'Didn't they tell you that?'

'They didn't tell me much.'

'I think they believe he did it just before he went to see you and the two of you went to the Plough and Sickle.'

'Not after he left there?' she asked.

'No, before.'

'You're sure?'

They were interrupted at that point by a waiter who handed each of them a menu large enough to be a protest placard, covered all over in a vast confusion of French, written almost unreadably in purple ink. But they were too absorbed in what they were talking about to wrestle with it, and unenterprisingly ordered shrimp cocktails and *escalopes de veau.*

'I'm not sure of anything,' Andrew said. 'But Marcus has admitted he went to see Miss Dunthorne and had a drink with her in the garden before he went to see you, and that after he saw you he went straight home, and the police seem to accept that.'

She nodded. 'He told me he'd just come from seeing Miss Dunthorne.'

'But he doesn't admit he had a row with her and upset the table and chairs and smashed some glasses, then chased her into the cottage and killed her.'

'I should think not!' she said. 'That's really what the police think? How silly can they get?'

'You're sure it's silly?'

She gave a deep sigh as if she were suddenly deeply weary of the silliness of the world in general.

'Look, I know Marcus,' she said. 'I can always tell if he's been in a row. He can't hide a thing. He's got a temper that bursts on you before you know it's there, it comes out of an absolutely clear sky, bang! And just what he'll do while it lasts is anybody's guess. It's frightening, with his size and all. But when it's over, it's over, and he gets the shakes. I think if he was a child he'd sit down and cry. He's always ashamed of himself and wants to make it up to the other chap. He goes round looking so like a whipped puppy it's quite comical sometimes. "Don't worry," you can say to him, "the other chap had it coming to him"—because Marcus doesn't often pick a quarrel, he's usually goaded into it by some fool who doesn't know what he's getting into. But it doesn't make any difference, you can't take his mind off it. He's got to apologize, and get the other chap to have a drink with him, and things like that. If he'd done a murder . . .!' She gave a sudden shrill little giggle, then clapped her hand over her mouth, shocked at the sound. 'What I mean is, if he'd had even a bit of a row, I mean just a few words with someone like Miss Dunthorne, I'd have known it the moment I saw him.'

'And you didn't notice anything unusual about him last night?'

'No, not last night.'

'But the other night—the night in the Sea Cave—you did?'

It was a mistake. She went dumb, sipped tonic and stared at the carpet. A few more questions from Andrew only met with silence. Then all of a sudden she appeared to take hold of herself and plunged into telling Andrew and Holly about the theatre, about how wonderful the people in it were to her although she knew they only thought of her as a kid, and how she had not known what it was to live until she had been taken up by them.

Not that she had any intention of staying in Helsington long, she said. It was wonderful experience she was getting, and she thought it would be worth her while to stay for at least a year. But then she was going to look about her. She sounded very confident and her chatter gushed in a swifter and swifter stream, sweeping aside Andrew's attempts at further questions. In a brief pause he suggested that it was time to go in to lunch.

They were on the way to the dining-room when they passed the Ladies' Cloakroom. That, at least, was what an illuminated sign on the wall called it. But it was not really a cloakroom at all. It was simply an alcove with a rail along it with a number of coat-hangers hanging from the rail, a shelf above the rail, and a notice stating that the management accepted no responsibility for any articles left there. There was no attendant. Loraine stood still abruptly as they reached it. Holly thought that she wanted to hang up her anorak, but it was something else that had made her stop. She was pointing at a coat on one of the hangers. It was of a light, rough tweed in dark blue and white with small flecks of red in it.

'Look at that, it's hers!' she exclaimed in a half-whisper. 'I know it. She was wearing it the last time I saw her. I'll bet she's in the dining-room. Oh God, perhaps I oughtn't to go in!'

'Whose is it?' Holly asked.

'Miss Chard's. You know—the dramatist. She's got a cottage in Roydon. She's—oh, she's wonderful. She saw me in a village show—she only went to it because I asked her to—and she asked me if I'd like to meet the Market Theatre people, and she fixed it up for me, and every time she meets Grandma in Roydon she stops and asks how I'm getting along.'

'Then why shouldn't you go into the dining-room just because she's there?' Holly asked.

Loraine shifted from one foot to the other. A number of thoughts seemed to be chasing one another chaotically behind her remarkable eyes.

'I wouldn't want her to think I was following her around,' she said. 'You know—being a nuisance when she's already done so much for me.'

Whatever her real reason was for not wanting to meet Lisa Chard, Holly was sure that that was not what it was. But she said, 'You needn't even speak to her. You're with us. She hasn't rented the dining-room.'

'Won't you talk to her, then?'

'It depends on whom she's with. We don't want to be nuisances either. I've only met her once before in my life.'

'But perhaps she'll come over and talk to you.'

'If she does, it's her look-out, isn't it? All you need do is look modest and self-effacing.'

'All right,' Loraine said, but with obviously real reluctance. 'Anyway, perhaps I'm wrong. Perhaps it isn't her coat.'

They went into the dining-room.

Lisa Chard was there, wearing a dress that matched the coat, with a brooch of sapphires and small diamonds pinned to it. To make things a little difficult, she was alone. However, she did not look in the least as if she wanted anyone to talk to her. She was at a corner table and although she looked straight at the three of them as they came in, her slightly cross-eyed stare gazed blankly through them, and she gave no sign of having recognized them. She had an empty coffee cup in front of her, a crumpled napkin and her bill. If ever a woman looked as if she wanted to be left alone with her thoughts, she did.

They sat down and a waiter brought them their shrimp cocktails.

A moment later Lisa mashed out the cigarette she was nervously smoking, stood up, left some money on the table and went towards the door. She was much paler than she had been the evening before and there were circles of shadow round her eyes, as if she had not slept. There was an air of deep depression about her. Holly thought that she was going to walk straight past their table without even a greeting, but at the last moment, when she was almost past, she paused, came to them, and standing beside Holly, put a hand on her shoulder in a gesture that was probably meant to be comforting.

'Hallo, Holly,' she said in her husky voice. 'Hallo, Andrew.'

She simply ignored Loraine. It could not have been accidental, and Loraine, Holly realized, was not surprised. But her face went white and she gave Lisa, a brief, bitter glare which did not match at all with what she had just been saying about her. Picking up her spoon, she looked down into the pink depths of her shrimp cocktail as if it were a crystal in which she was trying to read her future.

'Doing a little detecting?' Lisa said. 'Watch out with that child. She has some funny ways. But perhaps you're only doing it to pass the time. I'm finding that difficult myself. I tried to do some work this morning, but I couldn't keep my mind on it for five minutes together. And I didn't want to be alone and I didn't want company. So I decided to take myself out to lunch. It hasn't helped. And I'm only an outsider who really knew Judy very slightly. So I can only make a guess at what it's like for both of you at the moment. If it would help at all, drop in on me whenever you feel like it. I'm going home now and I'll be at home all day. As a matter of fact, I—I'd be grateful if you came.'

Giving Holly's shoulder another vague pat, she left.

Through her teeth, Loraine said, 'And that didn't include me!'

Andrew looked at her curiously. 'What have you done to her?'

'Ask her!' Loraine hissed.

'Don't you know?'

'No, I don't. I only know she doesn't like me any more. Here am I, thinking she's the most wonderful person in the world, and that's how she treats me! I think someone must've talked to her about me—told her lies. Perhaps your mother. She hates me, of course, because of Marcus.'

'I don't think my mother would have told anyone lies about you, all the same,' Andrew said.

'Someone else then. Someone who's jealous of the way she took me up. I have lots of people jealous of me for all sorts of reasons. I expect I always shall. I'm that sort of person. I'll have to get used to living with it. Perhaps Miss Chard is jealous herself. All I know is, she's turned against me, so when I saw her coat out there, I thought I'd sooner not come in.'

Intrigued, Holly said, 'Why should Miss Chard be jealous of you, Loraine?'

Loraine delved among her shrimps and brought out a spoonful.

'A middle-aged woman like her, you never know, do you?' she said. 'Grandma says it's her Time of Life. Whatever's wrong with a woman over forty, it seems to me, people say it's her Time of Life. That sounds to me just like a wonderful alibi some women think God's given them for being bitches, and I do know Miss Chard used to get snippy with me if even Mr Floyd stopped to chat with me, and she's got no real use for him, she just likes to keep him tagging along, and she still liked me at that time. That was when I was working for her, to help Grandma last Christmas when her veins were bad, and as I said, I thought Miss Chard was the most wonderful person I'd ever met. But she can't stand having anyone's attention on anyone but her. Then too, she's a failed actress, did you know that? She only took to writing those plays of hers after she hadn't made it on the stage. So perhaps she's jealous of me because of that.'

She was perfectly serious. Holly wondered if that was the right recipe for success. Perhaps Loraine's utter certainty that she was to be envied by all, was a success already, was going to the top, would actually get her there. If it did not, it would destroy her. The middle path, along which most people crowd their way sufficiently contentedly, was one that she would never be able to endure.

'About the Sea Cave,' Andrew said.

Loraine's face went empty. 'Well?'

'What was there unusual about Marcus that evening?'

'I didn't say there was anything unusual,' she said.

'I thought you did.'

'I only said there was nothing unusual about him last night.'

'When you went to the Plough.'

'That's right—except that he drank two whiskies, when

he usually sticks to beer, and he was a bit drunk and angry too when he left. That's because I wouldn't agree to back him up about what he says happened in the Sea Cave.'

'Are you going to tell us about that?'

The waiter brought them their *escalopes* and Loraine began on hers before she answered. Even then she only said, 'I did say it was sort of complicated, didn't I?'

Andrew agreed that she had.

She ate a little more.

'You see, I've told the police I don't know anything about what happened that night, and I can't very well go back on that, can I?'

'Can't you?' he said. 'If it wasn't the truth.'

She squirmed on her chair and said defensively, 'I don't see why I shouldn't look out for myself. Everyone has to. That's what Grandma said, and she made me promise I wouldn't talk to anyone about that night. And if I was only thinking of myself I wouldn't be here now, talking to you. And if I tell you the truth, you won't believe me.'

There was a little edge of desperation on her voice that sounded real. She swung round on Holly, for the first time bringing her fully into the conversation.

'No one would believe me, Miss Dunthorne. Some people would think I was trying to shield Marcus, though I don't know why I should. There's nothing between us, nothing serious. Honestly, you've no idea how young he is for his age. And some people like you would think I was just looking out for myself, saying I didn't see anything. But I didn't, I didn't! I didn't see anything at all!'

'But you were there, weren't you?' Andrew said. 'Even if you didn't see anything, you were there.'

'All right, I was there for a little while,' she said, 'but I'd gone to the toilet, you see. That's all. We got to the place and I said to Marcus, "I'm going to the toilet", and he said, "Right, I'll wait for you in the bar", and I went to the toilet and then I spent a bit of time on my face and hair—my wig, that's to say. I'd got a fabulous new wig, only four pound ten, kind of copper colour, something like the colour of Miss Chard's hair, and nobody'd seen me in it yet, except just Marcus. And that was why nobody recognized me. There happened to be no one in the powder-room I knew, but there must have been people around outside I did, but they didn't recognize me.'

'And that's what's made it so easy for you to say you weren't there,' Andrew said. 'The fabulous copper wig.'

'It was Grandma's idea.' She sounded aggrieved, as if she bore a grudge against chance for putting the temptation to lie in her way. 'She said, "You can't help Mr Marcus by saying what you saw—you'd do him harm, if anything—so you just say you stayed at home with me and I'll back you up, and he can say he stayed at home too, and that'll help to keep everyone out of trouble." And of course, I didn't want to get into trouble, just when everything's so wonderful . . .' Her voice trembled slightly. 'But I've been feeling terrible since I've had time to think. I'm fond of Marcus, even if he is just a scatty kid, I am truly. But now it's too late to help him, isn't it? If you keep changing your testimony, nobody believes anything you say. And anyway, I *can't* help him, because I didn't see anything.'

Holly's *escalope* was congealing on her plate. It was about three times as much as she felt like eating.

'I don't understand how you managed not to see anything,' she said.

'Because,' Loraine replied, 'only just after I came out of the powder-room, Marcus came straight up to me and said, "We're getting out of here!" I asked him why, and he said, "It's one of those nights and we're keeping clear of it." I didn't argue, because I knew what he meant. He meant there were two or three chaps inside who only go there when they feel like stirring up trouble, and they'd probably been drinking already, and Marcus knew there was trouble coming.'

'What was Marcus himself like when he said that?' Andrew asked.

'What was he *like* . . .? Oh, I see what you mean. You're thinking about how I said he gets the shakes when he's been in a row. You're wondering if the row had happened already when he came out.'

'That's it, more or less,' Andrew said.

'Well, he was in a state all right,' she said. 'He was angry about something. I've always thought it was just because he saw a nice evening being spoilt if we stayed—because, of course, there was that trouble he was in before, which meant he'd got to be extra careful if he didn't want the police to pick on him if anything happened . . . Oh, I don't know. I can't honestly see Marcus kicking an old man when he was down on the floor. I'd say, if he did, it was by mistake, he was trying to kick someone else who'd been asking for it. But there are people who say they saw him do it.'

She finished the last scrap of *escalope*, french-fried and boiled frozen broccoli that had been on her plate and gave Andrew an uneasy, placatory look, as if afraid of being told that she had not yet earned her lunch.

'Several people say it, you know,' she said. 'All I can say is, I don't think he acted as if he'd done something really violent when he joined me and said, "We're getting out of here!" He was excited and angry, but not as if he'd been in a fight.'

'These people who say they saw him kick the old man—who are they?' Andrew asked.

She was vague. 'Just people standing around.'

'Has Marcus any enemies that you know of?'

'*Enemies*? How could a boy like Marcus have *enemies*?' She made it sound like a disreputable disease.

'That's what I was hoping you might be able to tell me.'

She went into a state of deep thought, while her plate was removed and some crême caramel put down before her.

'Enemies,' she repeated, picking up her spoon. 'There's Fred, the barman, who doesn't like Marcus because of the time he helped to smash the place up. Then there's Kevin, who used to be my boy-friend and thinks I gave him up for Marcus, which I didn't, I only gave him up because he's no good, he's never going to get anywhere. Then there's Garry, who's a Communist, and says Marcus is just a rich layabout. Then there's Sonia, who went to work on Marcus and hasn't ever forgiven him because she simply couldn't make him see her. And there's Carol—'

'That's enough,' Andrew said. 'It's obvious Marcus lived surrounded by enemies who'd perjure their souls to get him into trouble with the law.'

'Only I wouldn't call any of those *enemies*,' Loraine said. 'They're all quite nice kids, really. Except perhaps Fred. He's got it in for Marcus because of the other time, when Marcus really scared him, and everyone saw it. Fred's never forgiven him that.'

'And a little here, a little there,' Andrew said, 'and a picture could be built up . . . Loraine, can't I persuade you to go to the police and tell them exactly what you've just told us?'

'They wouldn't believe me—not now,' she said. 'And if you *must* know,' she added, as if making a great concession to an unreasonable demand, 'there's a chap I've been seeing a good deal of lately. His name's Maurice and he works at the theatre—and he's insanely jealous, much worse than Kevin, and I'm afraid of what he'd do to me if he knew I'd been out with Marcus when I'd promised him I wouldn't. And then there's Grandma, saying, "Keep your mouth shut." So it's easiest to take the line of least resistance, so to speak, and tell the police I was at home all evening.' She took a quick look at her watch and exclaimed, 'Oh, my God, I must fly. If I've said anything to help, I'm glad, but I don't suppose I have. It was all in confidence, of course. If you tell the police what I've said, I'll say you've twisted everything, and gave me a good lunch to try and bribe me, and put words in my mouth and confused me till I didn't know what I was saying. Thanks for the lunch. It was fabulous.'

She sprang to her feet and shot out of the room.

Holly and Andrew sat there for some time after she had gone, both of them giving up any pretence of eating. The dining-room was fairly full and noisy, but Holly had the feeling that she and Andrew were huddled together on a little island of troubled silence.

After a little she asked, 'Do you believe in Maurice, Andrew?'

'He exists,' he said. 'We saw him. He ordered liver sausage.'

'Yes, and pickled onions. But his jealousy, does that exist?'

'I have my doubts.'

'But then what's her real reason for turning against Marcus?'

'I wish I knew.'

'She seems quite fond of him in her way.'

'I know.'

'And I've a feeling there's more to it than just wanting to keep out of trouble herself. I don't believe that would worry her in the least.'

'No.'

'And I don't think any orders from Mrs Gargrave would influence her in any way whatever.'

'I'm sure they wouldn't. It's more likely Grandma who's taking the orders.'

'Then what *has* Loraine got against Marcus?'

'Perhaps it isn't against Marcus. Perhaps it's our family in general.'

'But why?'

'God knows.' Looking depressed, Andrew beckoned to the waiter for the bill.

Holly had not thought of stopping at Cross Cottage on their way back to Roydon Saint Agnes, but when they reached the cottage they saw that the same police car that had been there before lunch was still in the road. The front door of the cottage was open.

'I wonder what they're doing there,' she said.

'Want to go in and see?'

'No . . . Yes . . . I think I'd like to.'

Andrew stopped the car and the two of them went into the cottage.

Mr Ditteridge was just coming out of the kitchen. In his impersonal way, he looked pleased to see Holly, as he might have if, in some game, he had just picked up a useful card in an otherwise unpromising hand.

'Miss Dunthorne, the person I wanted to see,' he said. 'I think you told me yesterday your aunt wasn't in the habit of keeping large sums of money in the house.'

'No,' Holly said. 'I don't think she ever did.'

'What do you think a maximum would be?'

'I don't know—ten pounds, twenty, something like that.'

'It would be unusual, then, for her to have as much as five hundred pounds in the house.'

'Oh, very unusual.'

'Yet she had it yesterday,' he said. 'She had five hundred pounds in five-pound notes stuffed into a tin in the kitchen. It's the tin in which she kept her coffee. There are coffee beans in it. And somebody knew that it was somewhere in the house. Last night a pane in the french window in the sitting-room was broken and someone got in and searched the place again. Perhaps it was the person who searched before, and perhaps someone else. In any case, it could be that that gives us the motive for her murder.'

# CHAPTER VII

Mr Ditteridge showed Holly the bundle of notes, though he did not let her touch them. They had picked up a strong scent of coffee from the tin in which they had been found. The scent had a peculiar effect on her, startling her out of the deep silence into which she at first retreated, as she usually did, when anger began to build up in her. Five hundred pounds for Judy's life. Was that all it was worth?

'No,' she said suddenly and loudly, 'not in the coffee tin.'

He had been talking to her up to that point, and she had not been listening. She had hardly been aware of the sound of his voice, though she had seen his lips moving. They had gone into the sitting-room, where the disorder was just the same as it had been the evening before, except that Judy's body had been taken away, and the rug too on which she had fallen. The space in the middle of the room was a bleak emptiness.

Andrew went to the french window with its broken pane, and stood looking out at where the green garden-table and chairs on the terrace were still overturned.

'Not in the coffee tin?' Mr Ditteridge said, picking up her line of thought very quickly. 'It shouldn't have been there?'

'No,' she said.

'She wouldn't have put it there?'

'Never.'

'Where would she have put it?'

'How should I know? But not in a ridiculous place like a coffee tin.'

'So we've two improbable things to consider,' he said.

'And sometimes one improbability leads quite naturally to another, and makes them both seem normal.'

'I don't understand.'

'Well, if she wasn't used to having sums like five hundred pounds in the house, mightn't she do something unusual with it? Mightn't she have felt that she'd got to hide it and put it in that coffee tin after all?'

'No,' Holly said.

'I think Miss Dunthorne's right,' Andrew said. 'Her aunt wasn't a nervous woman. She was used to living alone, and she didn't do much in the way of locking and bolting doors and taking a lot of precautions. I think, if she'd had five hundred pounds in the house, she'd simply have kept them in her handbag.'

'Suppose the money wasn't hers,' Mr Ditteridge said. 'Mightn't she have been extra careful with it?'

'You mean if she was looking after it for someone else?' Andrew looked questioningly at Holly to see how she felt about the suggestion.

She shrugged her shoulders. 'I suppose that just could be possible. Do you think she was looking after it for someone else?'

'It's just a wild guess,' Mr Ditteridge said. 'You seem so sure she wouldn't have had a sum of money like that in the house in the normal way.'

Holly's certainty began to feel less certain. People kept doing things that were quite unlike themselves, and often relations and close friends were the last people to notice it. They were too used to the person to bother about the little warning symptoms of something unusual going on under the surface.

She tried to remember if there had been anything unusual about Judy the evening before which she might have noticed if she had not been as absorbed as she had been in the thought of seeing Andrew again. She did not think so. Judy had seemed just her normal, talkative, affectionate, unworried self.

'I suppose it isn't *impossible* she'd have a sum of money like that in the house for her own purposes,' Holly said. 'But I think Mr Meriden's right, she'd have had it in her handbag, or perhaps in a drawer of her desk, or her dressing-table.'

'None of you drank coffee last night, did you?' Mr Ditteridge said.

'No,' said Holly.

'And you and Miss Dunthorne didn't have coffee earlier?'

'No, we had tea.'

'So there's no telling when the money was put into the canister.'

'Suppose,' said Andrew, 'it was put there last night, by the person who broke in, just to make you think what you're thinking.'

Mr Ditteridge turned weary eyes on him. 'If I was as sure of what I'm thinking as you seem to think I am, Mr Meriden, I'd be a much happier man than I am.'

'Oh, you'd thought of that,' Andrew said. 'Yes, of course, you had. I'm sorry.'

'No need to be sorry,' Mr Ditteridge said. 'It may be a useful idea. But I'm cagey about useful ideas, that's the truth. The danger lies in letting their sheer usefulness run away with you.'

He stood looking round at the open drawers and the books and cushions on the floor, as if he hoped that they would still yield him some admission that he had not been able to wrest from them yet.

'There's no knowing,' he repeated thoughtfully, 'when the money was put into the canister. That's one fact to bear in mind. But we need so many more. Haven't you any more to offer, Mr Meriden?'

A constable put his head into the room. 'Not a trace, sir,' he said and withdrew again.

'Not a trace,' Mr Ditteridge murmured. 'That's probably a fact too, though not as certain as the other.'

'No trace of what?' Andrew asked.

'A paper bag which, logically speaking, ought to be somewhere in the house or the garden,' Mr Ditteridge answered.

Holly felt the anger which had woken in her when she first saw the money, and which till then had had no object on which to vent itself, and so had only quietly eaten away at her nerves, come bursting out of her with calm-looking Mr Ditteridge as its target.

'Mystery is something I will not stand!' she exploded. 'Not one scrap more of it than we can avoid. What paper bag, for God's sake? What are you talking about, and why not tell us simply what you mean?'

'Why not? Well, only because I hadn't got round to doing it,' he said. 'I was just about to explain. The paper bag we're looking for is one that came from Cleeve and Coleford probably sometime yesterday morning. Their wrapping paper and their paper bags are quite distinctive. Those bright red and green stripes with the white spots dotted over them—they catch the eye. And Miss Dunthorne was seen carrying one yesterday in the Crown, when she went in there for lunch with Mrs Meriden.'

Cleeve and Coleford was the biggest general store in Helsington. It sold both men's and women's clothes, furniture, ironmongery, and almost everything else. If Judy had gone shopping in Helsington the day before, there was nothing surprising about her having gone into the shop.

'Why is that important?' Holly asked.

'Perhaps it isn't,' Mr Ditteridge said. 'It's just that we're trying to build up a picture of Miss Dunthorne's movements yesterday, and that paper bag's just an odd little thing that seems to have gone astray. It's faded out of the picture, leaving a little blank space. And I find that irritating, as I find it irritating if I know I've put a thing down somewhere and it isn't there any longer when I look for it. Probably it just means someone's seen fit to tidy it away, but still I find it irritating.'

'What's supposed to have been in the paper bag?' she asked.

'Ah, we don't know that,' he answered. 'We haven't the slightest idea.'

'Haven't you made inquiries at Cleeve and Coleford?'

'They're being made now. And since Miss Dunthorne had an account there, it's probable there's a record of any purchase she made. On the other hand, if it was something sufficiently small, she might not have bothered to have it charged, she might just have paid cash for it. But even if she did, we may still find out what it was, as she was well known in the shop.'

'Who saw her in the Crown with this paper bag?' Andrew asked.

'The girl at the desk. You pass it on the way to the restaurant. The reason the girl noticed it was that Miss Dunthorne had just left the Crown with Mrs Meriden, making some remark about the weather to the girl as she went out, because they knew each other slightly, then a moment later she came hurrying back and went to the Ladies' Cloakroom and left again, carrying the bag. She didn't speak to the girl this time, and seemed to be in a hurry.'

'If she could forget what it was so easily,' Holly said, 'it can't have been anything important.'

'Perhaps not,' Mr Ditteridge agreed. 'All the same, in a case like this, you never make up your mind beforehand what's important and what isn't. You just assemble every little piece you can find and then try to make a picture of them—like doing a jigsaw puzzle when you don't know what the picture's going to turn out to be. You've a lot of blue pieces, perhaps, and you think they're the sky, then they turn out to be part of a lady's evening dress, and come at the bottom of the picture, not the top.'

'What else do you know about Miss Dunthorne's movements yesterday?' Andrew asked.

'Most of what we know we know from your mother, Mr Meriden,' Mr Ditteridge answered. 'Mrs Meriden says she'd rung Miss Dunthorne about nine o'clock the evening before and asked her if she'd any shopping to do next day in Helsington, because if she had, would she like a lift, as Mrs Meriden was going in. Then she said she asked Miss Dunthorne if she'd have lunch with her, as she'd like a talk with her about her son Marcus, and didn't want it at home, where the other members of the family might come in at any moment. So Miss Dunthorne agreed, and Mrs Meriden picked her up about half past ten next morning and drove her into Helsington, where they separated to do their shopping, agreeing to meet in the bar at the Crown at twelve-thirty, which they did. They had a drink there, then went into the dining-room and had lunch, sitting over it till about two o'clock, then Mrs Meriden drove Miss Dunthorne home and dropped her here. And that's the last Mrs Meriden saw of her. So far as we know, Miss Dunthorne stayed at home for the rest of the day, working in the garden. Around four o'clock, Mr Floyd's told us, he telephoned her and said he was driving out to Roydon Saint Agnes later in the afternoon, and if she was going to be in he could drop in to give her this advice she wanted about the alterations to the cottage. He says she seemed pleased at the suggestion and though they didn't fix any special time for his visit, he thinks she probably expected him about six or six-thirty.'

Mr Ditteridge tugged at his long chin and looked away over Holly's head towards the terrace.

'Just why he didn't come, if that was the understanding, I couldn't tell you,' he said. 'He's vague about it himself. Says he and Miss Chard got talking and he didn't notice the time. Could be true. The vaguest things are often the truest.'

Holly thought of Stephen Floyd accusing Lisa Chard of not having let him leave when he should have, and of her contemptuous retort that he wasn't a child and could have left any time he wanted to. But perhaps she had known very well how to stop him.

Andrew went on, 'Do you know anything about Miss

Dunthorne's movements in Helsington yesterday after she and my mother separated?'

'Only a negative thing,' said Mr Ditteridge.

Holly did not understand. 'A negative thing?'

'Something she didn't do. She didn't go to her bank.'

'Oh,' Holly said. 'The money.'

'Yes, there's no record of her ever having drawn out a sum like that in cash. She paid most of her regular bills by cheque, and only drew out quite small sums for casual spending—just as you told me,' he added.

'There's something that strikes me as just very slightly odd in your story,' Andrew said. 'About that parcel from Cleeve and Coleford . . .'

'Yes?' Mr Ditteridge said.

'You haven't mentioned any other parcels. Miss Dunthorne had been shopping in Helsington, hadn't she? I don't know what she went shopping for, but I know when my mother does it, she comes back with armfuls of parcels. So wouldn't Miss Dunthorne have brought several with her into the Crown, when she arrived for lunch, together with the Cleeve and Coleford one? Or a shopping basket or something. And of course she'd have taken them out with her again when she left. So how was it that she somehow managed to leave just that one behind?'

Holly saw a sudden alertness in Mr Ditteridge's tired eyes.

'That's a point, Mr Meriden, a very good point. Though, of course, she could simply have dropped the parcel in the passage, and only found out she had after she'd dumped her other parcels in Mrs Meriden's car. Still, it's a point.'

'Do you know anything else about my aunt's movements yesterday?' Holly asked.

'Only what you told us yourself about your arrival here, Miss Dunthorne. And then there's what the boy Marcus told us about his visit around six-thirty.'

'What are you doing with him?' Andrew asked. 'Are you still holding him?'

Mr Ditteridge looked slightly surprised. 'We sent him home hours ago, Mr Meriden. We've no evidence against him, except that he came here and had that drink with Miss Dunthorne, which he's admitted, after being so foolish as to lie about it first. Then soon after seven he appeared in the Plough and Sickle with Miss Gargrave and had a couple of drinks with her and then he seems to have gone straight home. At least, between the time he left the Plough and the time Mrs Meriden says he got home, there was scarcely time for him to have done a murder. And in the Plough his behaviour was normal, except that he was in a bad temper with the girl, and drank whiskies instead of beer.'

'So it looks as if a second person came here and had a drink with Judy on the terrace after Marcus left,' Holly said.

'That's how it looks,' Mr Ditteridge agreed.

'Someone who thought she had that money and killed her when she wouldn't give it to him.'

He did not answer, but eyed her curiously, as if he were wondering if she were going to say any more.

When she did not, he observed, 'It's a pity about that paper bag from Cleeve and Coleford, because it distracts me. I keep on thinking about it and wondering why it isn't in a waste-paper basket, or the dust-bin or somewhere, when I ought to be thinking about that second person who came for drinks, or whether that brother of yours, Mr Meriden, is a much cooler customer than he looks, and could have gone to the Plough and put on a show of being nothing but a bit bad-tempered when he'd just done a murder.'

'Suppose,' Holly said, 'my aunt bought whatever it was she got at Cleeve and Coleford for someone else in the village, to whom she'd mentioned she was going into Helsington. People here often do that sort of thing. And that person might have come here and collected the parcel, paper bag and all, sometime after Judy got home.'

'That's a possibility.' He sounded enthusiastic. But of course, he had thought of it already. Holly heard that in his voice. 'An interesting possibility. I'd like some way of finding out if you're right, because, as I was saying, the thing distracts me when there are so many other important things to think about.'

But he did not really think the other things as important as the absence of the Cleeve and Coleford paper bag. For some reason he found that immensely significant.

Holly spoke of this to Andrew as they left the cottage soon afterwards and went back to the car.

'Why does that paper bag from Cleeve and Coleford matter so much?' she asked.

'I don't know,' he said, but absently, and she was not even sure if he had heard what she had said. She realized that he had not spoken since the superintendent had told him that Marcus had been allowed to go home. As he started the car he went on, 'I suppose you're thinking about Lisa. You're thinking that perhaps it was Lisa for whom Judy did some shopping at Cleeve and Coleford and that Lisa came to collect it in the afternoon, or even later, and that she's kept very quiet about her visit?'

'Couldn't that have happened,' Holly said.

'It could also have happened with half the people in the village.'

'Yes, of course.'

'But you think it was Lisa, don't you?'

'I didn't mention Lisa,' Holly said. 'It was you who did.'

They had reached the crossroads and turned to the right towards the old farm drive.

'Weren't you thinking of her?' he asked.

'Well, there's something odd about the way she and Stephen can't really explain why he was so late coming to see Judy,' Holly said. 'So suppose they did come, he to advise Judy about the alterations and she to pick up her package, and suppose they found Judy dead and decided to get out as quickly as possible. And then suppose they kept a watch on the cottage till they saw lights go up inside it—that's when I arrived—and then came along ever so casually to find out what was happening.'

They swung in at the gates of the drive.

'What you haven't said,' Andrew observed, 'is that perhaps they went to the cottage, one or both of them, and murdered Judy.'

'Because I can't think why they should,' she said.

'Hasn't it occurred to you,' Andrew said, 'that Floyd may have been late simply because he and Lisa were making love? People do, you know. It's a well known phenomenon.'

'But you said to me yourself you didn't think she was in love with him.'

'People have been known to make love to people with whom they aren't in love.'

'Well, don't sound so damned knowing about it,' she said. 'You don't actually know that that's what they were doing.'

'It's as good a hypothesis as yours.'

'Only I wasn't claiming my hypothesis was anything but a guess.'

'Nor was I.'

'Then what are we arguing about?'

'Are we arguing?'

'We're practically quarrelling.' The thought amazed her. 'Anyway, why are you still so worried about Marcus when the police have let him go?'

'I'm not,' he said.

'Are you afraid it's only temporary and that they'll arrest him again?'

'They haven't arrested him at all yet, as it happens.'

'No, of course not. But next time they really might. Is that what's worrying you?'

'I've told you, I'm not worrying about Marcus.'

'About the mysterious paper bag, then?'

'Suppose we say I'm just a worrier and leave it at that.'

They had reached the house. He stopped the car at the door.

'All right,' he said abruptly and turned to look at Holly, 'I *am* worried about Marcus, and in a way I'm scared that the police have let him go, because of you.'

'What on earth have I got to do with it?'

'Well, we'll find him at home now. How are you going to feel about seeing him? What do you think about him? What are you going to do?'

'I won't do anything special.'

'But how are you going to feel?'

'Just leave it to me,' she said. 'I'll manage.'

'You'll find the family standing solid behind him, you know, whatever any of them may be thinking in private.'

'Of course.'

'So if you aren't going to be able to stand seeing him, it would really be best to tell me now, and I'll get your case and take you to an hotel in Helsington—the Crown, or anywhere else you'd like to go.'

'I think I'd sooner stay here.'

He gave a little sigh of relief, and they went into the house together.

Marcus was not about. Holly went up to the room that she had been given and set about unpacking her suitcase, which she had hardly touched the evening before, apart from dragging out the few things that she had wanted for the night. She was hanging up the summer dresses that she would not need again that year when Kate came in.

She threw herself down on the bed and watched Holly for a little while without speaking. Like Holly, Kate was in slacks and a sweater. Her rich brown hair, instead of being swept up smoothly round her head, was hanging in a rather unbrushed mass round her shoulders. Her only make-up was an excessive quantity of green eye-shadow, which made her eyes look like caverns of grief.

'Holly, that offer you made yesterday,' she said after a moment, 'I mean, of a room in your flat—does it still hold?'

'Of course,' Holly said.

'You meant it? It wasn't something you just said without thinking about it or ever dreaming I might take you up on it?'

As a matter of fact, that was just what it had been. But Holly was not going to back out of it now.

'Come any time you like,' she said. 'The girl I've shared with for the last two years got married this summer, and I can't afford to keep the place on alone. But I haven't done anything yet about looking for anyone else. It's a slightly tricky matter, finding someone you think you're going to be able to bear to live with.'

'Do you really think you and I would get on all right?' There was unusual anxiety in Kate's tone.

'We ought to—we've known each other long enough,' Holly said.

'That isn't the same as living together, though. I might get dreadfully on your nerves. I get on most people's nerves, I think.'

'I might just as easily get on yours.'

'Oh, I haven't got any nerves.' Kate had stretched out on the bed and folded her hands under her head, but her eyes, deep in their green caves, were watching Holly intently as she moved about the room, putting her dresses on hangers, her cosmetics on the dressing-table and her shoes in the shoe-rack. 'I don't take enough notice of what's going on around me to have nerves. It's the observant, penetrating sort of person like Andrew who has them, not me.'

'Well, you can have the room, if you want it,' Holly said. 'But what's made you change your mind? What are you going to do when you get to London?'

'I thought I might go to a secretarial school. That's something I've never tried.'

'No more domestic science?'

Kate gave a slight shudder. 'You know, I can't think why I ever thought of it.' She paused, then added, 'I suppose you think I'm just running out on the family now that we're in trouble.'

That thought had crossed Holly's mind. But even so, she thought it was a good idea for Kate to get away from home.

'It isn't that, Holly,' Kate went on. 'It's just this feeling of desperation I have all the time. I feel I'm no use to myself or to anyone else. Take this trouble that's hit us now—I seem to be the one person who's quite outside it. Everyone else is doing something active about it, but I can't think of anything to do. I just look on and think how dreary it all is. And that's typical of how I feel about everything these days.'

Holly looked at the volumes of Chaucer at the bottom of her suitcase and decided to leave them where they were. She closed the lid of the case.

'Has Stephen Floyd got anything to do with this state of mind you're in?' she asked.

Kate closed her eyes, as if the suggestion filled her with extreme weariness. Then, without opening them, she answered, 'Yes, of course. Really, Holly, for a short time, I thought I'd found the thing that mattered. And he did too. I know that. Then Lisa Chard reached out for him and took him. I know you'll say, if it was as easy for her as that, then it can't have gone very deep with him, and I suppose that's true. All the same, if only we'd had a little *time* . . . I was crude, I suppose. I went after him much too obviously. And perhaps I didn't really attract him as much as I thought. But he did care just a little, I'm sure of that, and if only we'd had time . . .' She sat up abruptly, pushing back her tumbled hair from her face. 'I *hate* that woman, Holly. I'll agree with anyone who insists on saying so that she's generous and good-natured and kind, but I *hate* her.'

Holly had gone to the window and was looking out. She could see the roof of Cross Cottage among the beech trees that surrounded it. There was not even a tinge of autumn yet in their glowing green, which responded with gentle little shivers as the soft breeze stroked it. But in another two or three weeks, she knew, the green would be mottled with dull gold, then the gold, as it spread, would become patterned with warm copper, and that would darken to bronze before the leaves began to fall, leaving the branches in their lovely winter starkness.

She loved the patterns that trees made against the sky in winter. But she would not be here to see any of it. Cross Cottage would shortly be put up for sale and since it was a very desirable property would probably be snapped up at once by someone who was not too sensitive about the taint of murder. And Andrew, of course, would return to Canada, and Holly would probably never have the heart to come to Helsington again, but would stay in London. Working. Thank God for work.

She found herself feeling all of a sudden years older than Kate, instead of just the same age. Kate had had so much of what she wanted all her life. With a mother who was determined that her children should have all their needs and desires fulfilled, she had never had to learn to accommodate herself to frustration. But Stephen Floyd was something with which Isobel had not been able to provide her daughter.

'Oh, look!' Holly exclaimed.

'What is it?' Kate asked listlessly without getting up.

'Police.'

Kate shot to her feet and came to Holly's side in a couple of long strides.

A car had just come up the drive and stopped at the door. Mr Ditteridge and another man, whom Holly had seen in the cottage the evening before, got out and went to the door.

'Oh, no, no!' Kate said and with a great gulp burst into

violent tears. 'They've come for Marcus after all. Oh no, they can't have, it can't be true! It isn't true, Holly! I don't believe it!'

In a moment her face was all streaks of green eye-shadow, so that her eyes looked like those of some strange sea-creature, peering out through wavy strands of seaweed.

'Perhaps they haven't come about Marcus,' Holly said. She gave Kate a piece of Kleenex to clean up her face. 'Let's go down and see.'

Mopping at her cheeks, Kate fought the tears. For a moment she said nothing, but only mopped away and swallowed and stared fiercely at herself in the mirror, as if she felt a harsh and suspicious dislike of herself. Then, in almost her normal, indifferent tone, she remarked, 'I told you I was no use to anyone. Put a little pressure on me and I collapse. All right, let's go down.'

They went downstairs together.

They found the two policemen in the drawing-room with Isobel, Ben, Andrew and Marcus. No one took any notice of Kate and Holly as they came in. Mr Ditteridge was speaking to Isobel. At first Holly did not take in what he was saying, it seemed so senseless. It seemed that Isobel did not take it in either, for she only stared at him in a fixed, glassy way and did not answer. He repeated his question.

'But isn't it true, Mrs Meriden,' he said, 'that you went to your bank yesterday morning, just before you went to meet Miss Dunthorne in the Crown, and cashed a cheque for five hundred pounds?'

## CHAPTER VIII

ISOBEL WAS SITTING in one of the armchairs. Everyone else in the room was standing. Her stillness seemed unnatural. So did that unseeing stare that she kept on the superintendent's face. Stillness and steady concentration on another person had never been normal to her. She ought to have been on her feet, fidgeting about the room, turning quickly from one person to another, interrupting them when they spoke. Her rigidity looked like panic. It was like the freezing into immobility of one of those small, swift-moving creatures that go stiff with fright when something big and dangerous threatens them.

'Yes,' she said at last, 'I did. But I didn't know banks were supposed to give out that sort of information.'

Mr Ditteridge gave a small, deprecatory smile, as if he did not want to say too plainly that she was naïve not to have known better.

'It was also Miss Dunthorne's bank,' he said. 'We were looking into the question of whether she had cashed that sum herself.'

'No, I did,' Isobel said and paused, obviously not at the end of what she wanted to say, yet not quite certain if it would be wise to go on. She made herself withdraw her gaze from Mr Ditteridge's face and looked down at her hands, which were white from the tightness with which they were clasped together. 'Then I gave it to my husband. Why? Why is it important?'

'Because five hundred pounds in five-pound notes has been found in Miss Dunthorne's cottage,' he said. 'And if someone knew that she had that sum in the house, it might have been the motive for her murder.'

Isobel gave a stiff little nod of her head, still looking down.

'I drew it out in five-pound notes,' she said. 'And I gave it to my husband before going to meet Judy for lunch.'

'Isobel—' Ben began, then stopped abruptly. Holly was not sure if there had been warning in his tone, or simply bewilderment.

Isobel raised her head and smiled brightly at him, as if to reassure him.

'I don't suppose you're going to ask why I gave my husband that sum, are you, Superintendent? Certain things are allowed to remain private between a husband and wife.'

With words, she seemed suddenly to become her natural self, unclasped her hands, crossed and uncrossed her feet, shifted forward to the edge of her chair, as if she were just about to shoot up out of it, smiled brilliantly round at everybody and asked, 'But why are you all standing about like statues? Why don't you sit down? You're all looking as if I must have done something dreadful, giving Ben that money. I can't imagine why. It was a perfectly normal thing to do. As a matter of fact, it was for some new equipment he wants. I gave it to him in Helsington as soon as I'd got it from the bank. Ask him about it. Do sit down, Mr Ditteridge. And Ben—don't stand over me in that threatening way, as if you were thinking of strangling me. Do please sit down.'

Ben moved away from her and sat down in the middle of the long sofa, throwing his arms out along its back, so that he occupied the whole of it. His attitude had in fact looked threatening, when he had been standing close to Isobel, though probably it had only meant that he was startled and alarmed.

The rest of them found their ways to chairs, except for Mr Ditteridge, who seemed to prefer to go on standing.

'Mr Meriden, I suppose you haven't still got those notes in your possession,' he said. 'You couldn't show them to me?'

'No,' Ben said.

'You don't have to, of course.'

'I know that. But I couldn't anyway. I gave the money to Miss Dunthorne yesterday morning.'

Isobel started slightly and looked incredulous. 'But why, Ben?'

'Because she asked me for it,' he said.

'And you didn't ask her why?'

'No,' he repeated. 'I knew she'd return it.'

'And it seemed to you quite normal that she should ask you for a sum like that?' Mr Ditteridge said. 'In five-pound notes?'

'Why not? We're old friends. Very old friends. I was glad she felt she could come to me if she needed it. If she wanted it in cash, that was her business. Of course, it would really have been more sensible of her to go to my wife, but a lot of people take for granted that a husband handles the money affairs of a family.'

'The odd thing is, however,' Mr Ditteridge said, 'that Miss Dunthorne didn't need the money.'

Isobel cast her thin hands about in the air, as if she were weaving a spell. 'Ben, you should have told me . . .'

Mr Ditteridge went on, 'Her current account was in what I'd call a very healthy state. I wish mine were half as healthy. She'd about twelve hundred pounds in it. Then she'd a deposit account of a little over three thousand pounds, and investments on which she could have realized about seven thousand. And she can't have had many anxieties about the future, because she'd an annuity bringing her in fifteen hundred a year, which she bought with money left to her by her parents, and her writing brought her in at least as much as that again. And she appears to have lived quite modestly. There's a drawer in her desk in which she kept the monthly bills, and they add up to rather less than eighty pounds. So why, Mr Meriden, should she suddenly have needed to borrow five hundred pounds from you?'

Isobel made another fluttering gesture with her hands and turned to Holly.

'Have you any ideas about it, Holly?'

Holly shook her head. Andrew, who had been holding his in his hands, raised it and looked at her.

'I've an idea,' he said.

Ben began, 'Now, Andrew—' Then he decided not to go on, but fastened his heavy gaze once more on Isobel's face, as if there were some riddle there which it was life or death for him to answer.

'Isn't Loraine Gargrave at the bottom of it all?' Andrew said. 'Isn't it clear she said to Judy that she'd tell the truth about what happened at the Sea Cave if she was paid for it? And her price was five hundred pounds. And Judy let you know, Ben, that that was all she'd been able to get out of Loraine. So you said you'd pay up and you got Isobel to give you the money, and you gave it to Judy before she went to lunch in the Crown, so that she could give the money to Loraine that evening. And someone knew you'd done that. Someone knew that Judy had that unusually large sum of money in the cottage. And he went there, after Marcus had come and gone, and killed her for it. But then he couldn't find it, so he went back to look for it last night, and again couldn't find it. So the person we need to look for is someone who saw you hand Judy the money, or to whom you spoke about the deal with Loraine. Did you speak of it to anyone?'

Ben was not looking at Andrew, but had leant back on the sofa and was staring piercingly at the ceiling.

After a pause he said, 'I never said a word about it to anyone.'

'Am I right about the rest of it?' Andrew asked.

Again it took Ben a little while to make up his mind how to reply. At last he muttered, 'Near enough. I didn't want to say anything about it, even to Isobel, because, I suppose, it was bribing a witness. I don't know what sort of trouble one can get into for that and I didn't want her mixed up in it. But I was ready to do anything I could to get that wretched girl to tell the truth about Marcus. And the rest of it—that perhaps someone saw me give Judy the money, and killed her for it—that never occurred to me. I thought, of course, she'd already have handed the money on to Loraine.'

'How did you give Miss Dunthorne the money, Mr Meriden?' Mr Ditteridge asked. 'Did you just hand it to her in the street, a loose bundle of notes, or done up in a packet, or how?'

'It was in an envelope,' Ben answered. 'The one it was put into in the bank when my wife cashed her cheque.'

'So no one who saw you could have told that it was money?'

'No.'

'This envelope—you're sure it wasn't a paper bag from Cleeve and Coleford?'

So they had got back to the paper bag. Had Mr Ditteridge ever stopped thinking about it for a moment since Holly and Andrew had last seen him, she wondered. She saw Isobel make an abrupt little gesture with one of her thin hands, as if she wanted to stop Ben answering, but then she folded her hands together, sitting hunched in her chair, looking down at them, waiting.

'Quite sure,' Ben said.

'A paper bag,' the superintendent went on, 'which was obtained by you yesterday morning, when you went into Cleeve and Coleford to buy some handkerchiefs. Isn't that correct?'

Ben gave a sigh and did not look up. 'Absolutely,' he said.

'You see,' Mr Ditteridge said, 'while we were inquiring into any purchases Miss Dunthorne might have made, we stumbled on the fact that you went into the shop yesterday. But so far we haven't found any evidence at all that Miss Dunthorne went there.'

Isobel started forward in her chair again, her intent stare on his face. 'Why is this paper bag important?'

'Because we've a witness who says she saw Miss Dunthorne leave the Crown with you, Mrs Meriden,' Mr Ditteridge explained, 'then a minute or two later come back in a hurry and go out again, carrying this paper bag we've been talking about. Or anyway, a bag from Cleeve and Coleford. And now we can't find it, that's all. Which may not be important at all, but still it's odd. Do you remember if she had one with her?'

Isobel bent her head, pressing the tips of her fingers over her eyes, in the attitude of someone trying hard to visualize a half-forgotten scene.

'I'm afraid I didn't notice what parcels she was carrying,' she said. 'I think she had quite a number. And when we hung our coats up, she dumped the parcels on the shelf above them, saying there was nothing there to matter. I never leave parcels there myself. There's a notice saying the management doesn't accept responsibility for anything you leave there, and I prefer to take anything I'm carrying into the dining-room with me. But Judy didn't worry, and she put her parcels on the shelf. Then, when we left, we put on our coats and she picked up her parcels and we went out to the car. We were going towards it when she suddenly said she'd left something behind, and would I wait while she went back for it. I said I'd get the car out of the car-park and drive it round to the front and wait for her there. I did, and she came out of the hotel just about as I got to the entrance, and got into the car and I drove her home.'

'And the parcel she went back for, was it from Cleeve and Coleford?' Mr Ditteridge asked.

Isobel dropped her hands and looked at him with a new irritability, as if her readiness to co-operate were nearly at an end.

'Really, how on earth can you expect me to remember a thing like that?' she demanded. 'We all do half our shopping at Cleeve and Coleford. It's the biggest shop in Helsington. One gets so used to seeing those bags of theirs around that one simply doesn't notice them. But I'm sure she wouldn't have left a bag with five hundred pounds in it on that shelf. She'd have put it in her handbag.'

'So that means we've two bags to account for, instead of one.' Mr Ditteridge's tone said that he found the fact extremely tiresome. 'The one from Cleeve and Coleford that she forgot and came back for, and the one from the bank with the money in it, which was probably in her handbag. And come to think of it, there's a third . . .' He turned to Ben again. 'Would you tell me, Mr Meriden, what you did when you'd handed the money to Miss Dunthorne and she went off to meet your wife at the Crown?'

'I happened to meet Mr Floyd,' he answered, 'and we had lunch together.'

'Where did you go?'

'As a matter of fact, also to the Crown.'

Isobel's head jerked round in surprise. 'I didn't see you, Ben.'

'We went to the snack bar,' he said. 'I knew you and Judy wouldn't welcome us if we crashed in on you. You always liked having your gossip sessions on your own together. So when we saw you in the lounge bar, Stephen and I went into the snack bar and had beer and sandwiches.'

An explosion came suddenly from Marcus. 'I don't believe a bloody word of it! It's all bloody lies! There's no bloody sense in it!'

He reared up on to his feet, standing towering over the rest of them, flushed, excited and enormous. His voice had come bellowing through the room in a deep roar. He looked so huge and so splendid in his muscular perfection, and at the same time so defenceless, almost as if he might burst into tears in his childish bewilderment, that Holly wanted to reach out and pat him to calm him down, as if he had been some lion cub, not yet dangerous, but threatening to dig his claws innocently into the furniture.

'Five hundred pounds!' he bellowed. 'It's bloody nonsense! What do you think Loraine is? If you'd said five pounds, or ten . . . But even then, she isn't like that. She simply hasn't thought. She doesn't realize yet I'm in serious trouble. Once she does, she'll tell the truth. It's only because she thinks I'll simply be fined again, and you can afford to pay the fine, that she's holding off. And who wouldn't, in her place? It's no fun, going into court. People think you must have been involved in what happened. I don't blame her. But five hundred pounds . . .! Somebody's mad.'

'I agree the sum is a curious one,' Mr Ditteridge observed quietly.

Isobel was trying to behave as if she had not noticed Marcus's outburst. But her features had tightened, and her face, always rather colourless, was greyer than usual. Looking at Mr Ditteridge, she asked, 'What do you mean by curious?'

'Simply that it's a rather large sum for the girl to think of demanding,' he said, 'and yet, if there's something more serious involved than the Sea Cave affair, it seems rather small.'

'What do you mean by more serious?' she asked.

He shrugged slightly, as if he had not meant to be taken so literally.

'To return to those paper bags from Cleeve and Coleford,' he said, 'do you remember what you did with the one you brought home, Mr Meriden?'

'That *I* brought home . . .?' Ben said in a bewildered tone. Then he went on, 'Oh, you mean the one with the handkerchiefs in it. Of course. No, I'm sorry, I haven't the faintest idea what I did with it. But the handkerchiefs are in a drawer in my dressing-room. Do you want to see them? Shall I bring them down, or would you like to go up and take a look at them?' His tone had become sarcastic.

'I don't think that'll be necessary,' Mr Ditteridge said. 'But I would like you to try very hard to remember what you did with the bag.'

There was a silence. They all looked at Ben, though Isobel's gaze seemed to go through him, as if she did not see him. She gave the impression of being incomprehensibly terrified by the question that he had been asked and of waiting desperately and forlornly for help to come.

It came, if it was help, from Marcus.

'I remember about the bag,' he said.

Isobel gave a violent start. The rest of them turned their heads to look at him. He was still standing and was glowering so fiercely that Holly was suddenly able to imagine him knocking a man down and kicking him.

'I burnt it,' he said.

Isobel began incredulously, '*You* burnt—?' Then she stopped herself, clamping her lips shut as if she were scared of saying a word more.

'Why did you do that?' Mr Ditteridge asked mildly.

'Well, it was lying around,' Marcus said fretfully. 'In here. And the fire had been lit. At this time of year we always light the fire in the evenings. So I just threw the thing on the fire. That's all.'

'I see. Thank you.' Mr Ditteridge stood up. He was looking grimmer than Holly had yet seen him look, grimmer even than he had when he had just come from taking his first look at Judy's body.

It made Holly wonder if to him lying might not be something that he hated more than murder. It was what he was fighting day in, day out, the thing that hedged every other crime about, making impenetrable, prickly tangles around the small, hard core of ugly truth, which he could have dealt with swiftly and confidently if ever he had been able to get near it.

For Holly had no doubt at all that Marcus had lied, though why he had she did not understand at all.

With a curt good-bye to Isobel and Ben and ignoring the rest of them, Mr Ditteridge went away.

As soon as he had gone Holly saw taut muscles relax and expressionless faces become normal, and heard the small sounds, which go on in any room in which there are several people, start up again, making her realize how abnormally silent it had been until then.

But nobody said anything until Ben muttered that he was going to do some work, and if anyone wanted him, he could be found in the workshop. When he had gone, Isobel, almost soundlessly, began to cry, and Kate went to sit on the arm of her chair and began patting her shoulder consolingly, and Andrew walked to the far end of the room and stood looking out at the garden, and Marcus gave a queer shout of half-strangled laughter.

'God, when you think of it, it sounds just like blackmail, doesn't it?' he said with smothered, guilty-sounding mirth. 'Judy blackmails Ben and Isobel, and Ben gives Judy the money, then goes to the Crown to keep an eye on things from the snack bar, and Stephen Floyd, who'd seen the money handed over in the street, goes along with him, and goes to the cottage later and murders Judy to get it, and Lisa gives him an alibi, because he's her lover. Solution!'

Andrew turned on him furiously. 'Can't you keep your mouth shut, you bloody fool. You've made enough trouble for everyone already.'

'But I'm not serious,' Marcus said. 'First of all, Judy wouldn't blackmail anybody. Then Ben and Isobel wouldn't do anything for which they could be blackmailed. Then Stephen couldn't have seen the money handed over, because it was in an envelope. And anyway, he wouldn't commit a murder for five hundred pounds. And even if Lisa would give him a false alibi, if he wanted one, I don't suppose he does. Honestly, it was all nonsense. Just a bad joke. Sorry.'

'So you damned well ought to be!' Andrew blasted at him, white-faced.

'Now don't start pushing me around,' Marcus said. 'I don't like it and I won't take much of it. You've been doing it ever since you got home and it's time you stopped it.'

'Marcus,' Isobel said, having dried her eyes with abrupt little dabs with her handkerchief, 'you didn't really burn that bag from Cleeve and Coleford, did you? You never even saw one.'

'No,' he admitted easily. 'But he was making such a fuss

about the damned thing, I thought if I said I burnt it, that would make him shut up. Which it did,' he added with satisfaction.

'Oh God,' Isobel said and dropped her head into her hands. 'The way you tell lies. You don't seem to think it matters. Is it my fault? Have I always been wrong, trying to give you the happy sort of childhood I thought you ought to have, not always saying no, and don't, and you mustn't? I always felt so sure it was the right thing to do.'

'Of course it was, darling,' Kate said, patting her shoulder again. 'You've always been marvellous. And Marcus only said what he did to get the man off Ben's back. And after all, a paper bag—what an absurd thing to be making such a fuss about.'

All of a sudden Holly could not stand it any more. She had the feeling that everything that had just happened in that room had been a grotesque charade. Everyone there, she felt, had been playing a part, not being himself. Even she, saying nothing, had been involved in the strange play-acting, as the silent crowd, that at most murmurs 'rhubarb, rhubarb,' at appropriate moments. Going quietly out of the room, she went upstairs and started to pack her suitcase.

She left the house without anyone noticing her go. The suitcase was heavy, and by the time that she was half-way across the bracken-covered slope that she had to cross to reach the beechwood, she had to put the case down to rest. Dropping down on a patch of grass beside it, with the tall bracken standing up all around her, its scent fresh and subtle in the warmth of the afternoon sun, she asked herself why she had fled when she had and what she thought she was going to do with herself next.

The answer to the second question was simple. She was going to the cottage and she was going to stay there. Alone. The thought did not scare her. There was nothing she wanted quite so much just then as to be alone.

The answer to the first question was more complicated. What it came to was that she had been overcome by the feeling that no one in that room had cared about Judy. They had been desperately troubled by problems of their own, which Holly did not understand, or particularly want to understand. The feeling had been almost the same as she had had in Judy's study the evening before when Ben, Lisa and Stephen had been there together, a feeling that they were all concentrated on one another in a way that meant nothing to her, a feeling that she did not belong there. It hurt a good deal to recognize this. She had always taken for granted that she meant more to the Meridens than, plainly, she did. She had always assumed too that they cared for Judy almost as much as for any of themselves. But somewhere she had gone wrong.

She thought of Ben's almost contemptuous definition of friendship. '. . . the odd meeting from time to time, the occasional helping hand held out, a limited sort of trust . . .' And she began to think that perhaps that was all it was for people as they became older, compared with the ardent thing it was for a child. She murmured a few words to herself, '"I, a stranger and afraid, In a world I never made . . ."' Housman, wasn't it? A world in which one grew out of the friendships of one's youth and, if one were wise and the police would allow it, one returned to London as soon as possible . . .

She got up, grasped her suitcase again and went on.

She had to rest again twice before she reached the cottage. She still had the key to it that she had had for years. It was on the same key-ring as the key to her London flat. She went round the cottage to the lane and let herself in by the front door. She took her case straight upstairs to the room that had always been hers when she stayed there, and where she had made up the bed the evening before, and wanting to convince herself from the moment that she arrived that she did not mind being there alone, that that was indeed what she wanted, that she had come to stay, she unpacked immediately, completely and tidily, even taking the volumes of Chaucer out of the case and standing them on the mantelpiece, between two book-ends which at present supported an Agatha Christie, an Eric Ambler, the Oxford Book of Ballads and Brewer's Dictionary of Phrase and Fable.

The telephone rang.

She guessed who it was. It was one of the Meridens, probably Andrew, who had discovered her departure and was ringing up the cottage to find out if that was where she had gone. She was inclined not to answer. Then realizing that whoever it was might really be worried about her, and that even if she had had enough of the Meriden family for that day, she was being stupidly inconsiderate, she went downstairs.

The telephone stopped before she reached it.

She hovered beside it for a moment, wondering if she should ring the Meridens back and explain, with suitable apologies, that she had suddenly been overcome by an absolute necessity to be alone, saying that she hoped that they would forgive her. But she could do that presently. She went into the sitting-room and out through the french window on to the terrace.

The garden furniture had been put the right way up again. She sat down on one of the green chairs. It was warm and quiet in the afternoon sunshine. Yet there was a rim of dark cloud broadening above the tops of the beech trees, as if it might be going to rain later, as it had the evening before.

After a few minutes, Holly drifted into an undirected sort of thinking about the evening before. She tried to visualize what had happened out here before the rain started. Judy sitting here. Drinking sherry. Talking to Marcus. Telling him that he need not worry about his trial any more, since she was buying off Loraine Gargrave with five hundred pounds, and that the money was in the house for Judy to give to her. And Marcus thinking that he could use that five hundred pounds himself, perhaps to leave home, dodge his trial, disappear. And attacking Judy, killing her, hunting for the money, failing to find it, coming back in the night to hunt again. And being the one, this afternoon, who had refused, or had made out that he refused, to believe that Loraine would ever think of a sum like five hundred pounds as the price for telling the truth in court. Saying that once she had realized that he was in serious trouble, she would do it anyhow . . .

Very cunning, that, if he had not wanted it known that he had been told about the money by Judy or that he knew of its existence.

The trouble was that Holly did not believe a word of it.

But not to believe it was almost as difficult as to believe it, because it meant that in the very short time between Marcus's departure and the time when it had started to rain, someone else had come in, had sat out in the garden with Judy, had attacked her, upsetting the furniture, had chased her into the house and killed her. The search for the money, if that was what it had been for, could have happened after the rain had started, but not the struggle in the garden.

So it almost looked as if it had to be Marcus.

At least it was none of the other Meridens. Holly had talked to Ben in his workshop just as dusk was falling. He would not have had time to get to the cottage before the rain began and sit out here with Judy even for a few minutes. And Holly had found Kate and Andrew in the house and both had stayed there until Andrew had driven her home. And Isobel had come in and . . .

Holly felt the cold prickle of shock slide along her veins.

For Isobel had *come in* while Holly had been in the house. She had been out. To the village shop, she had said, and she had had an armful of groceries to prove it. But suppose she had come here to Cross Cottage as well, missing Marcus by a few minutes, and that some quarrel had blown up between her and Judy as they sat out here, and

Isobel had gone demented and done murder. Isobel, who right through the interview with Mr Ditteridge, had been suffering from some incomprehensible private terror.

The dark cloud had been thrusting its way steadily up the sky. It had just begun to cut off a little of the sunshine. With the shadow came a sense of moisture, just as it had yesterday. In another few minutes, Holly thought, it would be raining. She got up and went into the cottage.

Something happened to her then for which she had been half-consciously prepared, although she had been trying to pretend to herself that it was not going to happen at all. It was simply a sudden and violent assault by a sense of horror. It was the discovery that she could not bear being in the cottage alone. She fought it for a few minutes, turning on lights, because the room had darkened rapidly as the clouds spread, and drawing curtains, just as she had the evening before. But when she had done that she stood still in the middle of the little hall with the frozen feeling that she could not move from there, because there was nowhere in the cottage where she could bear to sit down and relax. Every part of it seemed to be tainted with the odour of violence. She caught herself listening in case there were any sounds that there ought not to have been. She seemed to feel a threatening presence behind her.

But when she looked, of course there was nothing there. And there was the telephone there, with which she could ring up the Meridens and ask if after all she could come back to them for the night. They would probably understand both why she had run away and why she wanted to come back. She nearly did it. But then she had a different idea. She went upstairs to her bedroom, put on a jacket, picked up her handbag, turned out the lights that she had just switched on, let herself out into the road and went up it through the rain that had begun to fall to the odd white house of Lisa Chard.

## CHAPTER IX

THE HOUSE STOOD some distance back from the road, with a strip of recently laid out garden in front of it. The grass had the look of only just having become a lawn, the roses were still meagre, the shrubs had not yet had time to develop. The strip was narrow, a mere cleavage through the old apple trees and brambles and briars. The garage was by the gate and only a narrow paved path ran from it to the house.

Inside the house lights were shining. As Holly approached it she saw Lisa Chard, through a great window that appeared to take up one whole side of a room, walking up and down it, then move to one side of the window and reach out to pull a cord to make the curtains swing together. As she was doing it, she saw Holly, gave her a small wave just before the curtains closed, and when Holly reached the front door, was there to greet her.

'Good—I'm glad you came,' Lisa said, making it sound as casual as if Holly had just dropped in to ask for her subscription to the Red Cross or to borrow half a pound of sugar. 'I'm alone and in a hopelessly frustrated state of mind. I thought I'd got myself so trained that I could do at least a small amount of work every day of my life, if I decided I would. But today I've torn up every single thing I've put on paper.'

She led the way into the big room where Holly had seen her the moment before. She was wearing a long pale grey kaftan made of heavy silk with a fine woven pattern in it that looked Chinese, and a pair of glittering green earrings. Emeralds, were they? She was holding a half-smoked cigarette between her stubby fingers. A big ash-tray on a coffee-table was so full that it was plain that she had had a day of chain-smoking as well as frustration. The coffee-table was an undistinguished piece of teak. It would be no loss when it was replaced by Ben's beautiful piece in sycamore inlaid with bog oak.

Holly liked the room. It was very restful and simple. Its walls were pale grey, the carpet was a darker grey, the hearthrug was a furry white thing in front of a small, very plain fireplace made of slate. The curtains, which, now that they were drawn, covered one whole wall of the room, were of a dull, faintly silky material in a deep grey-blue. The chairs were in different shades of green. A big pewter bowl of roses, very casually arranged, stood on a cabinet which Holly recognized as Ben's work. So the coffee-table had not been Lisa's first order.

There were very few ornaments, but what there were, a clumpy, Chinese-looking horse, a black goblet covered with delicately moulded figures, an enamelled vase, and one or two other things, somehow asserted to Holly's ignorant gaze that they were valuable.

The room lacked the dead-fish eye of a television set. There was no radio in it either, and no bookcase. In fact, all that Holly had against it was that it did not look as if anyone lived in it. Nevertheless, it would be a very fine place to walk up and down in, backwards and forwards, smoking cigarette after cigarette, when you happened to be feeling frustrated.

A log fire had been laid in the fireplace. Lisa went straight to it and held a match to the crumpled paper under the logs. Then, gesturing to Holly to sit down, she subsided, with her feet drawn up under her, on the hearthrug, and as the flames went leaping up the chimney, gave a little shiver, as if they had touched her with a chill.

'I like a fire on these autumn evenings,' she said, 'though I've got the heating turned on already. I simply can't bear being cold. But this is the only fireplace in the house. I told Stephen I had to have one. He was against it. He said the whole conception was wrong and that I'd find I never used it. But I do, I light it almost every evening, even when

I'm alone. In fact, it's just when I'm alone that I want it most, to sit and dream over. When I was a child a real fire in my bedroom, all to myself, was as far as my dreams of luxury went. All that I actually had was a gas fire, and I was never allowed to light that except when I was ill. Sometimes I used to light it in secret and sit and smoke by it in the middle of the night, particularly when I was a little older and coming home late from dances. But then I'd have to open the windows wide to let the smell of smoke out, so the room got as cold as ever. I hate open windows except when it's really warm. That's breaking one of the commandments, isn't it? "Thou shalt not sleep with thy windows shut". I always do. I told Stephen, "You needn't put a window in my bedroom at all, so long as you light it properly." But he said there was a bye-law or something against that. So I've got an enormous great window with double glazing and I never, never open it.' She came suddenly and very lightly to her feet. 'What would you like to drink? Sherry?'

She still had not asked Holly why she had come.

Holly said that sherry would be fine. She had just realized what it was that the colours of the room reminded her of. The grey, the green and the blue were like the green of downland, the blue of a cloudy sea and the grey-white of chalk cliffs. All quiet, serene and empty.

Lisa went to Ben's cabinet and took out glasses and a bottle of sherry. Holly found that it was very different from the terrible stuff that Isobel was forcing on her family at the moment. Lisa stood sipping it, looking down at Holly thoughtfully, then abruptly sank down on the hearthrug again, curling up as close to the fire as she could.

'I don't suppose we were actually so very poor when I was young,' she said. 'I don't really know. It wasn't the sort of thing they ever talked about if I was listening. So I've never known for sure. Was all the scrimping and saving necessary? Were they really rather noble to be doing it, to give me what they thought was a good start in life? Or was it just a state of mind from which they derived a good deal of pleasure? That was how I always used to think of it then, because they never explained anything to me. So one day I left the nice secretarial school where I was learning shorthand and typing and went off with a concert party that was just going off abroad to entertain our troops in Germany. I was as lousy an actress as you could find . . .' She broke off with a throaty chuckle, throwing the stub of her cigarette into the fire. 'I've got one of my talking jags on, haven't I? I've hardly let you say a word since you came into the house.'

'Go on,' Holly said. 'I've nothing special to say. It was just that I couldn't stand being alone in the cottage.'

'But I thought you were with the Meridens,' Lisa said.

'I couldn't stand that either.'

'No?' Lisa eyed her curiously. 'Ah well, there are times when strangers have their uses. Better the devil you don't know than the devil you do. That's true, you know. It's finding yourself intimate with the devil that's so frightening. You're going to stay the night, aren't you? Where's your suitcase?'

'At the cottage,' Holly said, 'but I didn't mean—'

'Of course you didn't, but I do mean I'd like you to stay. I'd be very grateful if you did. It may seem absurd to you, but I've been getting more and more scared all day, all alone here. You see, a horrible thought came into my head a little while ago. Horrible for me. Then I thought, it's just hysteria, and I do hate hysterical people, so I haven't said anything about it to anyone. But now you're here—well, tell me what you think. I suddenly thought, suppose Judy was killed in mistake for me.'

Holly was not at her brightest, and at any time might have found this difficult to follow.

'But there isn't the slightest resemblance,' she said.

'No, of course not,' said Lisa. 'But suppose the police are quite wrong that it was someone Judy knew who killed her, someone she had a drink with. Suppose there's some explanation they haven't thought of yet of how the table and chairs got overturned on the terrace, and that it was a stranger who broke in and killed her and ransacked the place. What was he looking for, that's what's so puzzling, isn't it? What was there that would bring a ruthless, professional criminal—because that's the kind of person I'm thinking of—to Cross Cottage? Judy didn't keep valuables around. *But I do*!' Her croak of a voice went up shrilly. 'This house would be worth ransacking. A man who knew what he was at could get away with thirty thousand or more. Now do you understand why I'm scared?'

'You think . . .' Holly felt cautious, and advanced by one short step at a time. 'You think some professional criminal came here to rob you . . . was given directions . . . a house close to the crossroads just before Roydon Saint Agnes . . . a middle-aged—that is, a woman of—'

'Middle-aged is correct,' Lisa put in. 'And a writer too, don't forget.'

'Well then, a writer living alone with a house full of precious things . . . and he came to kill her and take everything . . .'

Lisa gave a laugh that ended in a fit of coughing. 'You make it sound fantastic. Of course, it *is* fantastic. A professional wouldn't be quite so careless as to go to the wrong house and kill the wrong woman, would he? And in any case, he'd probably have taken pains to go there when the house was empty, so that he didn't have to kill anybody at all. Holly, I'm so glad you came. There are times when having no one to talk to makes one's brain do the most extraordinary things. Usually I like it. The uninterrupted company of the human race drives me nutty. But it happens to be true that this house is full of precious things. And I've never once felt nervous about it till today. I've always said to myself, everything's insured, what does it matter if something gets stolen? I've never thought, I've never realized, that I myself could be—vulnerable.'

Holly was confused, and so stayed silent. It was just

beginning to dawn on her how much she would like Lisa's explanation of why Judy had been killed to be true. Not that Holly wished Lisa any harm in the world. She did not want this professional criminal that Lisa had dreamed up to return tonight or any other night, to murder the right woman this time and to strip her house bare of the things she loved. But to be able to feel that there had been something impersonal in Judy's murder, something not so very much more human than the crash of a bus when she happened to be inside it, or the falling of a chimney-pot off a roof on to her head when she was passing in the street below, would slightly relieve the nightmare.

Lisa had lit a cigarette and was inhaling with quick, nervous puffs.

'I'm a fool for jewellery, you know,' she went on. 'I can't resist it. Any time I've some money to spare, I buy diamonds and emeralds and sapphires, and I deck myself out in them, even when I'm alone. I say to myself, why shouldn't I? It may be ridiculous, but it gives me pleasure. I never had any pretty things when I was young. And it's a good investment too. I never buy anything without advice. After all, who knows, the stuff I write could go out of fashion any day, and if I haven't saved and invested well, I could be right out in the cold again where I started. And I don't mean ever to be poor again. I've had that. And I'm not talking about my childhood now. That was drab, but not squalid. My first marriage is what left the scar. Going back to my dreary old shorthand and typing just to keep a roof over our heads while my dear husband painted the most Godawful pictures you ever saw. And I even persuaded myself I liked them and that some day he'd be appreciated by everyone, and I stuck it out till one day I looked at one of his paintings and said to myself that nobody—I mean *nobody*—was ever going to say it was anything but junk. So I daubed a big cross right across it in black paint, and took all the money we had in the flat, and packed a bag and left London and rented a caravan for a month, where

I lived on chips and wrote *The Lesser Evil* . . . I'm not a nice woman, Holly. I expect they've all told you that already. I do horrid cruel things to people, like painting that cross. That wasn't necessary. But it gave me enormous satisfaction. I've never regretted it. So nobody likes me for more than a little while. And don't look so distressed about it, darling. There are lots of people walking this earth whom nobody likes, and they don't die of it.'

Instead, somebody had died whom everybody had liked.

'I didn't know you were married,' Holly said.

'Twice,' Lisa answered. 'Marriage is one of the things that doesn't stick with me. The second time round was better than the first, in fact, the man was rather sweet, very affectionate, very hardworking, very loyal, and it was all my fault it broke up. I'd got into bad habits by then and couldn't settle down to being a good housewife, a good stepmother and fidelity. I ought never to have married the poor love, it wasn't fair. It was pure self-indulgence on my part—I mean, trying to make a daydream come true, that dream about marrying and living happily ever after, the sort most of us have at sixteen, but ought not to be playing with at thirty-six. So I made up my mind, never again, and now I have brief love affairs with houses. I build them, and live in them for a little while, and sell them. I'm very careful, of course, that they're all good investments. I haven't lost any money through any of my ventures yet.'

'Then you won't be staying here long,' Holly said.

'I'm not sure. Probably not. I haven't really thought about it. I'm in the middle of a new play, and when I'm working on a play I don't attend to much else.'

'Speaking of money,' Holly said, 'you don't know about what they found in Judy's house, do you?'

'Money?' Lisa said swiftly, almost jealously, as if it were a subject of which she had the monopoly.

Holly told her about the five hundred pounds that had been found in Judy's coffee canister, about how Isobel had admitted having cashed a cheque for that sum before her lunch with Judy, had given the money to Ben, and how he had given it to Judy to give to Loraine Gargrave.

'That girl!' Lisa exclaimed with a hoarse, almost admiring chuckle. 'Did you and Andrew get anywhere with her at lunch today?'

'Nowhere much.'

'I didn't think you would. I know her quite well, you see. I've been studying her. She's supplied quite a lot of the raw material of the play I'm writing. It's about a girl who comes out of a good working-class family, who gets taken up because of her talent by a bitchy character like me, gets involved with an innocent like Marcus, betrays every standard she's been brought up to, gets let down by the bitch, who gets tired of her, and ends up murdering the bitch and getting the boy blamed for it. I thought of it when she came to work for me last Christmas, when her grandmother's veins were bad. I think they got bad at Loraine's bidding, because she wanted to pick an acquaintance with me. I was amused at first and encouraged her, and I'll say this for her, she worked like a beaver while she was here. The house has never been so sparkling clean since. And when she persuaded me to go and see her act and I realized she really had some talent, I got her in with the Market Theatre crowd. I thought that was the least I could do for her, as by then I'd had my idea for the play. But the naïve little soul thinks that means she's almost at the top of the tree already, and thought she could hold me up for a part in the play, at least when it goes on tour, if not actually in London.'

'Hold you up?' Holly said, bewildered.

'Yes, she's rather inclined to blackmailing tactics.'

'But do you mean she *knows* the play is about her? Was she threatening you with libel or something if you didn't give her the part?'

A curious deep blush spread over Lisa's rather plump cheeks. She drew in a deep lungful of smoke and breathed it out slowly, watching it with concentration as it was drawn towards the chimney and faded up it.

'No . . . no, of course not,' she said. 'That was just a manner of speaking. She thought she could play on my feeling for her. She thought I *had* a feeling for her, instead of realizing that I'd been rather disgracefully exploiting her—listening to the phrases she used, you know, getting her opinions on anything from abortion to the colour problem. And, of course, sex. Always and especially sex. But she didn't realize it was all going down into note-books, and she hasn't read the play. Even if she did, she wouldn't recognize herself. I've changed all the superficial things, and mixed her up with one or two other people, and completely altered the circumstances, and made it all terribly North Country and urban. No, that doesn't worry me.'

But something did, and something was wrong with that explanation. Lisa was still not meeting Holly's eyes, but had gone on watching the trail of smoke.

Holly asked, 'Is all this conversation we're having going to go down into notebooks?'

Lisa looked round at her then with a warm, brilliant smile. 'Well, naturally, darling. Absolutely everything I hear, everything that happens to me, goes down on paper before I forget it. I've drawers and drawers full of the stuff. But you haven't been saying very much, have you? So you needn't worry. I've been doing all the talking. Now what about tonight? You can't possibly stay alone at Cross Cottage, so if you don't want to go back to the Meridens you'd better stay here. Just wait a minute till I get some clothes on, then we'll go along and get your case. And as I said yesterday, my spare room's always ready, because I get a good many random visitors, and I've a cold chicken and some salad and we'll open a bottle of wine and a tin of rum babas, so you see you won't be any trouble at all. Here, have some more sherry while you're waiting.' She put the bottle down beside Holly and hurried out of the room.

Holly was in a passive, acquiescent frame of mind, in which it seemed natural to do what she was told, so she had some more sherry. The result was that when she and Lisa presently walked along the lane she was in a faintly drunken state. Normally two sherries would not have had this effect on her, but what with emotion and weariness and the drinks that she had had at lunch-time, her world had been tending to revolve around her anyhow. The sudden coolness of the rainy evening outside, after Lisa's very warm sitting-room, made it worse. Not that it worried her. She began to think it might be a good idea to drink a great deal too much and spend the rest of the evening in total stupor.

Lisa had changed into the clothes in which Holly had seen her the evening before, the green jersey dress, the mackintosh, the gumboots. She had a plastic rainhood over her reddish hair. Holly had brought no coat with her, but Lisa had found a nylon waterproof for her to wear. They hurried along the lane as fast as they could and were only half-way along it when Holly saw that there were lights on in the cottage.

'Police again,' she said.

'I suppose it *is* police.' Lisa stood still.

'Who else could it be? Who else would turn on lights?'

'Then where's their car?'

That was certainly a point. There appeared to be no car anywhere near the cottage.

'If you'd sooner wait here . . .' Holly started off boldly.

'Don't talk nonsense,' Lisa interrupted her. 'I only came because I didn't like the idea of letting you come along here alone.'

She trotted on again, and was ahead of Holly when they reached the door of the cottage.

Holly took the key out of her handbag and fitted it into the lock. At the sound of it someone inside came quickly to the door, someone whose footsteps were far lighter than those of Mr Ditteridge. Holly pushed the door open and saw Andrew.

'So that's where you went,' he said, looking past her at Lisa. 'Why couldn't you let us know? We've all been going crazy with worry.'

Perhaps because the unexpected lights in the cottage had scared Holly more than she wanted to admit, she turned bad-tempered.

'What are you doing here?' she demanded. 'How did you break in? You've no right to be here. What do you mean, going round turning on lights, behaving as if you owned the place?'

'I didn't have to break in,' Andrew said. 'Someone did that last night, remember? So all I did was put a hand in through the broken window and unlatch it. And I turned the lights on because I was looking for you.'

'If I'd been here, I'd have turned on the lights myself, shouldn't I?'

'God knows if you would or not.' He sounded as irritable as Holly. 'I've been ringing up every ten minutes or so, and I came to the house once and banged on the door and didn't get any answer and didn't see any lights and went away again. Then I thought I'd better come back and find out for sure if you'd gone into hiding, or really gone away, or—or come to any harm. For some reason I didn't think you might have gone to Lisa or anywhere else in the village. I think you might have let us know what you meant to do. Bolting off like that without a word to anyone wasn't exactly kind. At a time like this it's easy to—to exaggerate one's worries.'

Lisa thrust one of her strong little paws through Holly's arm and squeezed it.

'If you marry him, darling,' she said, 'you'll find him very protective and jealous, which is probably how it ought to be. Not, as you'll have gathered, that I'm an expert. But I'm sure it's a good sign that he's been driven mad by horrible visions of you battered to death, rather than sitting down happily to play his Bach records, or whatever his recreation is. And since he's here, he can carry your suitcase for you. She's spending the night with me, Andrew, so when you're ready, you can bring her and her case along with you.'

She turned briskly away into the darkness, setting off towards her home.

Andrew looked after her with a black look on his face. 'How I hate tact! Anyway, what made you go to the damned woman? What did we do?'

'You were all thinking so hard about yourselves, and not about Judy, that I couldn't stand it a moment longer,' Holly said. 'And I felt you were all telling lies! Every one of you. I was sure they were lies.'

'What lies did I tell?'

'I can't really remember. But if you didn't, then all the others did.'

'And you lump me in with the others, do you? I've no identity of my own.'

They had drifted into Judy's study, and Holly had sat down in the chair at the desk. Andrew remained standing in the doorway.

'Is that all I am?' he asked. 'One of the Meridens, the family you wanted to belong to? The same as Kate and Marcus?'

She did not answer at once, but picked up a pencil and began to roll it backwards and forwards on the desk. After a moment Andrew made a grab at the pencil and threw it into the wastepaper basket.

'What lies did I tell?' he repeated.

'You were silent when the others told lies,' she said. 'That's almost the same thing.'

'What lies did they tell?'

'I can't remember clearly any more. I'm just a bit drunk, I'm afraid. People keep giving me drinks, and on the whole it's very helpful, but now I'm in a muddle. Marcus admitted he lied about that paper bag. And Ben told some awful lies I don't understand about giving that money to Judy to pay off Loraine. And Marcus made up his silly story about blackmail, as if blackmail was a joke. And you—don't you understand, Andrew, you went away? That's what you did. You just went away four years ago, without ever asking me what it meant to me, or if I wanted you to go, or telling me when you'd come back, or anything—anything at all. And now you think you can walk back into my life, just when you feel like it, and take up where we left off—as if I'm still a child—as if I'll still do anything you tell me. Whereas . . .' She paused. That was a good solid word. She liked it. It brought her down to earth, checking the feeling that had been growing in her that she might float up to the ceiling. '*Whereas*,' she said with even more emphasis, 'I am an adult. I am very mature for my age. Everyone says so. I am not to be swept off my feet by a passing emotion. I . . . I am . . . I am not . . .' She seemed to have forgotten what she had set out to say, and picking up another pencil, began to roll it backwards and forwards on the desk.

'Whereas,' Andrew said, his voice quite changed, having lost all its simmering anger and become very gentle, 'going away without asking you to go with me was the silliest thing I ever did in my life. The question remains, will you go back with me when I go away again?'

'No,' Holly said, 'of course not.'

He reached for her, took her by the arms and drew her to her feet. He held her close to him.

'Yes,' he said.

'No.'

'You don't know what you're saying, my love, you're drunk, you just said so.'

'All the more reason for you not to take advantage of me. This is a time for very sober thinking.'

'I'm not trying to take advantage of you. I'm talking to you for your own good. Mine too, of course!'

'Oh, can't you understand, Andrew?' She drew away

from him. The room was even unsteadier than it had been before. 'We're strangers now. You said so yourself this morning. I don't know you. And I never have. I was a child when you went away. Just eighteen.'

'That's nothing nowadays. Women almost have grandchildren at that age.'

'Then you should have taken me away with you then.'

'Granted.'

'Oh, listen. When you went away I accepted it in the way children do accept the disasters that happen to them. They know these things just happen and they've no control over them. They take the shock and start to think about something else. But of course they don't forget them, and they never quite trust the person who's done it to them—even if they love them.'

'Don't you trust me?'

'You're a stranger,' she said stubbornly.

'People sometimes fall in love with strangers.'

'I think it's probably an awfully dangerous thing to do.'

'You've grown awfully cautious since I used to know you. You're as strange to me as I am to you, but I've fallen in love with you.'

'Since when?'

'Since long ago. But you kept me waiting a long time, didn't you, while you did your growing up? But why do you think I came back, if it wasn't to find you again?'

'Wasn't it to see your family again? I thought I was just an incidental.'

'It's the family who were incidental.'

'I don't think I quite believe that.'

She was arguing against herself, because all that she seriously wanted just then was to be held in his arms again and to feel that there was nothing else that mattered. But it was true that the memory of that old hurt had lingered on and done more to her than she had ever really realized before.

'And now I'd better be going back to Lisa,' she said. 'My suitcase is upstairs. I must go and pack it.'

'Why not come back with me?' Andrew asked.

'Lisa's expecting me,' she said. 'She's nervous, you know. Really quite scared. She's worked out a theory that Judy was killed in mistake for her. She's afraid some gang are after her jewellery, and got mixed up between the two woman writers living near the Roydon crossroads.'

'It's a nice theory,' Andrew said. 'It might even be correct.'

'What about the five hundred pounds then?'

'It would simply mean that everything Ben said about that was true, the money was for Loraine, and that in fact it had nothing to do with the murder.'

'Except that Judy wouldn't hide a bundle of five-pound notes in a coffee canister. It just isn't like her. For one thing, she'd have been afraid they'd spoil the coffee.'

He began to laugh. 'All right, go and pack, then I'll take you along to Lisa.'

By the time that they reached Lisa's home, they found that she had carved the cold chicken and made a salad and opened the tin of rum babas and also a bottle of claret. Lisa asked Andrew to stay, but he answered that he was expected at home, and went away into the darkness. Lisa had laid the meal on a trolley which she wheeled into the sitting-room, and she and Holly ate sitting by the fire, while Lisa talked a great deal, mostly about her impoverished childhood and her two marriages and the play that she was working on now. There was no doubt about it, she thought it an extremely good play, and Holly in her muzzy way, managing to stay only just this side of sleep, was quite ready to believe her. How could someone with so much simple faith in herself not be right? She wondered what it felt like to have that kind of faith. She knew that she would never have it.

It did not seem to worry Lisa that Holly hardly ever

answered her. The sound of her own voice, going huskily on and on, seemed to be keeping something at bay for her, some nervousness, some genuine fear. Perhaps, Holly thought, she really believed in those jewel thieves and that they might return. If they had, Holly would not have been much help. As soon as the two of them had had the coffee that Lisa made presently, Holly went up to her room. After the little one in which she would have slept if she had had the courage to remain at Cross Cottage, it looked huge, exotic and luxurious, with a sea-green bathroom opening out of it. She had a deep, very hot bath, in which she wallowed until the water began to cool, then fell into bed and was asleep in seconds.

She did not wake until nearly nine o'clock next morning. She could smell coffee and bacon. Tumbling out of bed, she got dressed in a hurry and went downstairs. As she reached the bottom, the doorbell rang.

From the kitchen Lisa called out, 'Holly? Be a dear and go and see who that is, will you? I've just started on the eggs.'

Holly went to the front door and opened it.

Ben stood there. He strode into the house as if he did not see her, and went straight to the kitchen. He had neither shaved nor combed his hair that morning. There were red rims to his eyes. His walk seemed more crouched than usual, more shambling. His arms swung heavily at his sides, as if he were preparing to hit out violently at someone.

'Lisa, do you know anything about Isobel?' he demanded.

'Isobel?' She turned a startled face to him. She was standing at the stove, basting the eggs that she was frying. She was wearing a rather frayed-looking dressing-gown of yellow quilted nylon, and for once no jewellery.

'Yes, Isobel!' he shouted at her. 'Have you seen her? Have you heard from her?'

'No,' she said. 'Why should I?'

'No reason. None. It was just a hope. She's gone.'

'Isobel's gone?'

'Isn't that what I'm telling you?' He made a queer groaning noise that sounded like a mixture of rage and misery, and suddenly, as if his legs would not hold him up any longer, dumped his heavy body down on one of the spindly plastic chairs. 'In the night sometime. Got dressed and went away. And hasn't taken anything with her. No luggage. Not even a handbag. No money either, so far as any of us can tell. Just gone. Vanished. And didn't even leave a note behind her.'

## CHAPTER X

LISA SLID TWO fried eggs on to a plate that had two rashers of bacon on it and put the plate down on the table, where a place had been laid with knives and a fork, a large breakfast cup and toast and butter. She picked up a coffee pot that she had been keeping warm on the stove and filled the cup. She looked entirely concentrated on what she was doing.

'Come along, Holly, breakfast,' she said.

Whatever else happens, the young must be fed, that was what her attitude stated.

Holly was hungry. The coffee smelt delicious, and the eggs were just as she liked them.

'But why come looking for Isobel here, of all places, Ben?' Lisa went on.

'I suppose because I didn't know where else to go,' he said. 'And sometimes it helps, talking to you.'

'I thought those days were over,' she said. 'You've made it so very clear they were.'

He kneaded his two big hands together and muttered, 'Yes—yes.'

'Did you by any chance want to make sure that I hadn't disappeared mysteriously too?' she asked. 'That I was—in normal health?'

'What else are you ever likely to be in?' he asked. 'You know so well how to take care of yourself.'

She gave a wry smile as she picked up a half-empty cup of coffee from the counter-top beside the stove, drank what was left in the cup and refilled it.

'Even I am not indestructible,' she said. 'I have been known to suffer.' Turning, she leaned against the counter-top, and looked at him with her piercing, cross-eyed gaze. 'What happened?'

'What happened—?' Ben gave a start. 'Oh—about Isobel.'

'Concentrate, Ben,' she said with reproof in her voice. It sounded as if she were reminding him that they had an audience and that he should be careful what he said. 'Have you had any breakfast?'

'Yes—not really—it doesn't matter,' he mumbled. 'But I'd like some coffee.'

She reached for a cup and saucer in a cupboard and filled the cup with black coffee and added three spoonfuls of sugar. She seemed to know how he liked it. 'Well, go on.'

'I don't *know* what happened,' he said. 'I think it was about midnight when we went to bed. I felt dog-tired and I went to sleep at once. I don't know when Isobel got up. I'm used to not waking when she gets up. She's always slept badly and she's had a habit for years of getting up quietly and going wandering about the house in her dressing-gown, making herself a hot drink and reading for a time and so on. She didn't take pills if she could help it, though the doctor often told her she'd be better, less wound up, less subject to anxiety and depression, if she would. Anyway, last night she must have got up quite soon after we went to bed, because her bed was hardly disturbed. And that's all I can tell you. She seems to have got dressed in what she was wearing yesterday, a skirt and a jumper, and put on a waterproof, and gone out. Her handbag, the one she usually uses, was in the hall, with a good deal of money in it. None of her other clothes seem to be missing. That's going by what Kate said. I'm not observant about things like clothes. Isobel could have taken half of what she possessed away with her, and I don't suppose I'd know for sure whether or not she had. But Kate's been going through her things, and says there's nothing missing but just what Isobel had on yesterday.'

'Then doesn't it sound,' Lisa said, sipping coffee, 'as if she suddenly felt she had to go for a long walk by herself, and that's all? You don't need to take money or luggage for a long walk? Aren't you getting very upset over nothing?'

'But what a crazy thing to do,' Ben said. 'Do you think she's as crazy as that?'

'I don't think it's all that crazy—if you've a reason for doing it.'

'What reason had she?'

'A need to think.'

'On a rainy night like last night? And she'd the whole house to think in.'

'But houses are full of ghosts that interrupt one.'

'Oh, for God's sake! And it's past nine o'clock now. She's been gone for seven or eight hours. And even Isobel wouldn't go a seven or eight hour walk in the rain. And just suppose she did, she'd have left a note, you know. "Gone walk—don't wait breakfast."—that sort of thing. She's very considerate always.'

'How do you know she's been gone as long as that?' Lisa asked. 'She might have stayed in the house, making her hot drinks and reading, until morning, then decided it wasn't worth going back to bed and gone for a walk instead. It had probably stopped raining by then. So she may simply have thought it would make her feel better to get out into the air. She may even be home by now.'

Ben gave her a stare of pure amazement. 'Believe it or not, I never thought of that!'

'And perhaps didn't want to think of it.'

He came to his feet. 'Can I telephone, Lisa? Can I ask them if she's got home?'

She gestured to him to go ahead and he left the kitchen in a hurry.

In a minute or two he was back.

'No,' he said, 'she hasn't got home.'

'Then hadn't you better tell the police?' Lisa said.

'Do you think I ought to?'

'Yes.'

'But if it's nothing . . . If she really did what you suggested . . .'

'And if she didn't?'

He flopped down on to the chair that he had left a few moments before and looked at her with the bewildered, rather childish air of someone waiting to be told what to do.

'The police,' he said. 'You think I ought to call them now, not wait a little?'

'Now, Ben. Don't wait.'

'But if it's nothing . . .'

'Then it won't have done any harm. With one murder on their hands already, they'll understand it if the people involved aren't too rational in their behaviour.'

'One murder—*one* murder!' Ben's voice went strident. 'Why are you telling me you think Isobel could have been murdered?'

'Well, she could have committed suicide. That's what you're really afraid of, isn't it?'

He lunged to his feet again. 'All right, I'll call the police straight away. But you're crazy, Lisa. It couldn't be murder.'

'We've already had one murder that couldn't have happened,' she said. 'No one could have wanted to murder Judy. Everyone's agreed on that. I'd face the fact that it could have happened again.'

'No.' He made a gesture with one hand as if he were brushing cobwebs away from his face. 'No. Not this time.'

'Of course, if there's anything you *know* . . .'

'There isn't. God, you're cold-blooded, Lisa. How I ever thought otherwise . . .'

'My blood's cold only when it's been chilled,' she retorted with a sudden little spurt of venom in her voice.

'All I know is, Isobel's vanished,' he said.

'Go and call the police then.'

'All right, I will.'

He went out again.

Lisa gave Holly a contemplative look as if she were wondering how much of all this she had taken in. Holly kept her face as wooden as she could, reached for the marmalade and spread some on her toast and butter. She was thinking hard about a number of things that had only been hazily in her mind before. One of them was that if, as now seemed to her fairly certain, Ben for a time had been Lisa's lover, then that explained a great deal about the atmosphere in the Meriden household, the sense of strain and suspicion, the unnaturalness with which they had all been behaving.

Anyway, it did if Isobel and the others knew about the love affair. Holly wondered if they did. It was possible, of course, that in a family like the Meridens you were expected to have love affairs if you felt like it, and to talk about them without concealment. Yet Holly did not think so. She thought that to Isobel at least the solidarity of the family unit was the most important thing in life and that the discovery of Ben's infidelity to that ideal would be an overpowering shock.

Holly had to admit that she was profoundly shocked herself. She was accustomed to the love affairs of her contemporaries and she knew theoretically that people of Ben's and Lisa's ages were still capable of having them, but it did not seem at all proper to her that they should, at least if they happened to be people whom she knew. However, she suspected that there was something not very adult in this attitude, and she was not going to let Lisa see how she felt. She knew that it would amuse her. She seemed to be amused anyway, because when Holly did not respond to the questioning look in her eyes, she gave a crooked little smile and turned away to pour out more coffee for herself.

The front door bell rang.

'Damn!' Lisa said viciously. 'That's Stephen.'

Carrying her cup, sipping from it as she went and not hurrying at all, she went out to the hall.

'For God's sake, Stephen, not *now*!' Holly heard her say impatiently, and deduced that he had attempted to kiss her. Lisa added, 'Ben's here, phoning the police. Isobel seems to have disappeared.'

What Holly noticed about Stephen Floyd's answer was its lack of incredulity, even of surprise.

'She has, has she?' he said. 'When?'

'In the night sometime.'

Lisa brought him into the kitchen, asking, 'Have you any cigarettes? I've finished mine.'

He held out a packet and she helped herself. He nodded to Holly and sat down. Lisa gave him a frowning look.

'Were you expecting it, Stephen?'

'I was expecting something to happen, I didn't know what,' he said.

'Why?'

Before he could answer, Ben returned. He looked disconcerted when he saw Stephen, hesitated for a moment in the doorway, then muttered, 'They're sending someone out. I'd better get home. Are you coming, Holly?'

'Let the child finish her breakfast in peace,' Lisa said, 'then she can go over to you presently, if she wants to.'

'All right,' Ben said. But he remained standing where he was. 'Stephen, has Lisa told you about Isobel?'

'Yes, I'm terribly sorry you've got this worry,' Stephen said with coolly unconvincing sympathy.

'You can't think where she could have gone—you haven't any ideas?'

'I'm sorry, no,' said Stephen. 'Have you tried her other friends in the village?'

'Kate's been telephoning them, one after the other. No one knows anything.'

'I'm sorry,' Stephen said again.

Lisa went to Ben and patted him on the shoulder. 'Leave it to the police, Ben. They'll know how to set about finding her, if she doesn't just turn up by herself. There may be some quite simple explanation.'

Without answering, he turned away, and a moment later Holly heard the front door open and slam behind him as he went out.

Lisa turned on Stephen. 'Why were you expecting something to happen to Isobel? Go on, why?'

He was watching Holly eating toast and marmalade, as if it gave him satisfaction to see something so normal happening. Instead of answering Lisa, he said to Holly, 'So you were here last night—a bodyguard for Lisa. How lucky for her.' His glance went back to Lisa. 'You're really very afraid of Isobel, aren't you, darling? Scared stiff.'

'Of *Isobel*?' she said. 'I got nervous, I admit that—wouldn't you, if you were living alone so close to where there'd been a murder? And wouldn't you be glad of company? But to be afraid of Isobel . . . Why were you expecting something to happen to her, Stephen?'

He gave the small smile that only just moved his lips and did not seem to touch any of the rest of his sharp-featured face.

'Are you sure you want me to talk about it with Holly here?' he asked.

'I'm afraid there isn't much Holly doesn't know already,' she answered.

He shrugged his bony shoulders. 'Wasn't it obvious, then? Sooner or later Isobel was certain to find out about you and Ben, and what'd she do then . . . Murder? Suicide? Losing her memory? Disappearing? What's the odds?'

'But even if she might—just might—think of murdering

me, you can't seriously suspect her of murdering Judy?' Lisa said, though with something uneasy in her voice, as if she were not as unconvinced as she sounded.

'I've suspected her ever since it happened,' he answered.

'In God's name, why?'

'I was with Ben in the Crown the day before yesterday when Isobel and Judy came in for lunch. I saw them together.'

'What's that got to do with it? Were they quarrelling?'

'No, but Isobel looked terrible. I thought she was ill. I've never seen her so pale. And she spilt her drink and had to get another, her hands were shaking so badly.'

'Did she know you and Ben were there?'

'I don't know. I saw most of it in that big mirror in the snack-bar. And so did Ben. He watched them all the time. And he wouldn't leave when I did, but looked as if he meant to stay till the women left. Incidentally, if he hadn't got a fairly good alibi, I'd take for granted it was Ben who murdered Judy. He's got the best motive of anyone I can think of. If Judy was blackmailing him by threatening to tell Isobel about his affair with you—'

'*Blackmailing*—!' Holly began furiously, but choked helplessly over a mouthful of toast.

'How would Judy know of it?' Lisa asked quietly.

'From the Gargraves, of course. The thing had just begun, hadn't it, it was at its most passionate, wasn't it, just about the time Loraine was coming here to work for you, to help her grandmother out? And apart from the fact that you never bother to conceal much, you've got your awful habit of actually making notes about everything that happens to you, and Loraine, I should guess, is a nosy little thing. She may even have taken some of your jottings away with her. You'd never notice, because I don't believe you ever give a second glance at what you write down.'

Lisa gave a deep sigh. 'It's true, quite often I don't. Just writing the thing seems to be enough to fix it in my memory.'

'You need something to help you fix your love affairs in your memory, do you?'

'Oh, don't be a fool. It's the odd things people say that I write down, the unexpected, irrational things they do that tell one so much about them . . . But Stephen, we aren't talking of Ben murdering Judy, or of Isobel murdering me, either of which would make sense—'

'They would not!' Holly broke in wildly. 'Judy wouldn't have blackmailed anybody!'

In a very gentle voice, as if he wanted to be particularly kind to her, Stephen said, 'But just suppose she did, Holly. Last night that man Ditteridge came to talk to me. He asked me a lot of questions about Ben and Judy. He'd heard the old gossip. He asked me other questions too . . .'

Holly was so angry that she went into one of her choking silences.

He went on, 'I seem to remember saying to you that people change as they grow older. They don't always stay as nice as they were when they were young. And just think of her, a lonely woman, unmarried, repressed, in love with Ben herself, actually engaged to be married to him at one time. Think of her finding out that he was having an affair with Lisa. With Lisa, not with her. If he was going to be unfaithful, why shouldn't it be with her? Mightn't jealousy of Lisa drive her to take revenge on him by threatening to tell Isobel all about it? The money she asked for might be quite a small part of it for her. It would be her feeling of power that would give her satisfaction, the feeling that any time she wanted to, she could pay him out for what he'd done to her.'

Holly was still dumb with rage. If there had been a good blunt instrument handy, such as a poker, or even a Japanese bronze vase, she might have hit out at him with it. To make things worse, Lisa began to laugh. Holly's rage engulfed Lisa too as she listened incredulously to the deep, hearty laughter.

'So the five hundred pounds they found in the cottage

was the blackmail Ben paid her, to stop her telling Isobel about me, and he borrowed the five hundred pounds from Isobel herself to pay the blackmail! Stephen darling, you need your head examined.' But Lisa went on laughing, as if she found something exquisitely comical about the idea. Then she sobered abruptly. 'But we aren't talking about Ben, we're talking about Isobel. Isobel wouldn't murder Judy because Judy was blackmailing Ben by threatening to tell Isobel about his affair with me.'

'No,' he agreed.

'Then why?'

'Jealousy, of course.'

She shook her head. 'You still don't make sense.'

'But it's so obvious.' There was great patience in his voice, as if he were explaining something to the singularly dim-witted. 'Everyone knows Ben was in love with Judy before Isobel, and that he only changed over to Isobel because she had money, and he couldn't go his dedicated way in life without someone to support him. And everyone thinks the two women have been so wonderful about it, accepting the situation and becoming great friends—'

'Whom do you mean by everyone?' Lisa interrupted.

'Well, what I mean is, the story's around. It's considered one of the interesting legends of the place. I'm relatively a stranger, and I live in Helsington, not in Roydon Saint Agnes, yet I've been told it in the local pubs more than once.'

'I see,' Lisa said, as if the thought did not please her. 'I wonder what they say about me.'

'Better not inquire. But to go back to what I was saying, suppose Judy and Isobel weren't really as wonderful as all that. Suppose that all these years there's been the knowledge at the back of Isobel's mind that Ben had loved Judy more than he ever did her—after all, when they were young, Judy must have been far the more attractive of the two—and suppose Isobel had always had the knowledge that it was really her money he'd wanted. All right, she puts up with it, because he's given her most of what she wanted, a family, a kind of prestige she's proud of, the sense of backing him in work she really admires, and so on. But would you say she's ever given the signs of being a happy, satisfied woman? Not to me. I've always thought I've never known a woman who lived more desperately on her nerves. And all her progressiveness, her understanding, her tolerance, that she's made such a parade of, hasn't that just been a constant reminder to herself not to let her own jealousy get out of hand for a moment—because it would ruin her whole life if it did? And then you come along.'

Holly said, 'She had Marcus on her mind. Judy told me so.'

Neither of them looked as if they had heard her.

'You're right about one thing,' Lisa said. 'It was Loraine who talked about Ben and me. But I think it was to Isobel, not to Judy. As a matter of fact, Loraine actually threatened me. When she wanted a part in my play, I was so tactless as to laugh at her, and she told me I'd be sorry for it, because she knew so much about me she could spoil my life for me here in Roydon. I didn't take much notice. I thought it was just temper. But just about then I noticed that I wasn't welcome at the Meridens' any more, and that Isobel had a way of discovering there was something on the other side of the street that she simply had to attend to at once if she saw me coming.'

Holly remembered then that Lisa had spoken the evening before of how Loraine had tried to hold her up for a part in her play. Lisa had said that Loraine was inclined to blackmailing tactics. But at that time Lisa, with the strange, deep blush that Holly remembered, had avoided letting her know what it was that Loraine had held over her.

Lisa went on, 'I've wondered if the trouble over Marcus wasn't Loraine's revenge on Isobel, if Isobel laughed at her when Loraine told her the story about Ben and me. Because you can be sure, whatever Isobel believed, she wouldn't have given it away to Loraine. With her immense sense of dignity, she'd never have given away what she felt.'

'How long ago did you have this trouble with Loraine?' Stephen asked.

'About a month, I think. It was just a little while before the row in the Sea Cave.'

He nodded thoughtfully. 'I think I'm right then. Isobel had just about long enough to brood on what she'd found out to go hopelessly out of her mind. And remember, we don't know what Loraine may have told Isobel about Ben and Judy. We don't really know, do we, what there was to know? But perhaps Loraine did. Her grandmother had worked for Judy for years. If Ben and Judy had actually had an affair—'

Holly stood up with a violence that rocked the kitchen table. It was only luck that the cup from which she had been drinking did not go rolling on to the floor and smash. She bent over the table and shrieked at him.

'You're talking beastly, horrible nonsense! You don't know any of the people you're talking about! You're just making things up to enjoy in your own horrible malicious way! None of it's true—not a word of it!'

He gave her a patient smile. 'These things happen, you know.'

'Not to Ben and Judy.'

'All right, all right,' he said, as if to placate her. 'Not Ben and Judy. But do you know what you remind me of? The child who was told the facts of life and who answered that though such things might happen in some families, they certainly didn't in his.'

'Stephen, be quiet!' Lisa said sharply. 'The child's been through enough.'

'Sorry,' he said. 'But these young things who think they know everything . . .' He gave a shrug to show how much they bored him.

Holly walked straight out of the kitchen and out of the house.

She had no particular plan in mind, except to get away and calm down, and as she walked towards the road she had not even made up her mind where she wanted to go. She did not want to go to the Meridens, she did not want to go to Cross Cottage. She thought for a moment that she might take a bus into Helsington and take a room for herself at the Crown. But stalking out of Lisa's house all of a sudden, as she had, she had not brought her handbag with her, which meant that she had no money for the bus fare.

She might have gone back into the house to fetch her handbag, but just for the present she did not want to do that either, for if she saw Lisa, she would probably apologize for Stephen and try to persuade Holly to stay, and she would have to pretend she'd got over her rage when she had not. In the end, with her hands in her pockets and her head drooping, and kicking a stone ahead of her aimlessly as she went, she turned towards Cross Cottage.

She was almost there when she saw a familiar, solid figure approaching from the village, looking just as if she were coming to do her usual cleaning at Cross Cottage. Mrs Gargrave was wearing a neat navy blue coat, a blue and white headscarf, knotted under her chin and the surprisingly high-heeled shoes in which she generally went about her business in the village. When she saw Holly, she waved and began to hurry, as if she were afraid that Holly might go away. She was panting a little as she arrived at the cottage door, where Holly had waited for her.

'Oh, Miss Holly, I'm glad I just caught you,' Mrs Gargrave said. 'The milkman said you were staying with Miss Chard. She took an extra pint because of you, he said. He said he was surprised, seeing he thought you'd be staying with Mr and Mrs Meriden. "Well, Mr Grove," I said, "I can't see it's any business of yours where she chooses to stay. You talk too much," that's what I said, "and I've no use for talk." But all the same, I was glad he told me, because ever since yesterday, when you and Mr Andrew came to see me, I've had something on my mind, and at last I made up my mind I'd come and see you and tell you all about it. So I was going to Miss Chard's. But if we can go in here and talk in private, I'd like it ever so much better. And I can pick up my slippers too. I've been wondering about them. I'll have to look for some other work soon, so I'd like my slippers.'

For as long as Mrs Gargrave had worked for Judy, she had always left a pair of old slippers in the cottage, into which she had changed every morning when she started work. In public she would never have allowed herself to be seen except in the smart sort of shoes that she was wearing now, but in her own home or for work, she favoured flat-heeled bedroom slippers. Judy had sometimes said that as long as the slippers were there, safe in the broom-cupboard, she knew that Mrs Gargrave could be counted on, even when her veins were at their most troublesome, to return to her eventually. That the slippers now were to be removed felt to Holly something incredibly final, the true and sad end of what had been a quite fruitful human relationship.

'All right, let's go in,' she said, 'but it'll have to be by the garden door. I haven't brought my key with me.'

She led the way round the cottage.

As they went, Mrs Gargrave said, 'It'll only take a minute, what I've got to say.' This sounded very unlikely, for nothing that Mrs Gargrave had ever had to say had taken only a minute. 'It's just that I got to thinking after you and Mr Andrew left, and last night I couldn't sleep with thinking. I lay in my bed and I tossed and I turned. I lay on one side, and then lay on the other, and all the time I thought, I've got to go and talk to someone, because now everything's different, I can see that. It isn't just a little matter of a fine and then everything being forgotten, it's different, and I'll have to talk about it to someone.'

'It's about Marcus, is it?'

The path round the cottage was wet from the night's rain,

and the late roses in the garden were still spangled with raindrops. The earth had the fragrance of wetness and there were puddles in the seats of the green metal garden chairs on the terrace, which now had been set right way up.

Holly slipped a hand through the broken pane in the window and reached for the latch.

'That's right,' Mrs Gargrave said. 'I tossed and I turned and I lay on one side and then on the other and I couldn't stop thinking, because I never meant any harm to come to Mr Marcus, of course. You'd know I'd never want that. It's just that I thought all he'd get would be a fine, and his parents could easily afford it, and it wouldn't make any trouble for him, just teach him a lesson which maybe wouldn't do him any harm, while standing up in court to have mud slung at her could do Loraine a lot of harm—'

'Oh, stop,' Holly interrupted shrilly. 'Oh God—look!'

She had just pushed at the glass door, across which, to her surprise, the curtains were drawn, and had thrust with one hand at the curtains before she had withdrawn the other hand from the hole in the glass. That was why, when she saw the pair of eyes looking at her across the semi-darkness of the room inside, that hand jerked, and she felt a sharp stab of pain as the jagged edge of glass cut her wrist.

The eyes were unwinking and steady. Isobel Meriden lay on the sofa, with cushions arranged comfortably under her head and her hair spread out untidily over the cushions. Her shoes, which were muddy, had been put neatly side by side on the floor near the foot of the sofa. She had taken them off, either to be comfortable, or thoughtfully to avoid soiling the cretonne sofa-cover. On one of the small Victorian tables near her were a glass, a half-bottle of whisky, which was nearly empty, and a pill-bottle, which was entirely empty. A sheet of paper with some writing on it and a ball-point pen lay on the floor near the sofa.

Dripping blood from her cut wrist on to the doorstep,

Holly stood rooted where she was. It was Mrs Gargrave who crossed the room, tip-toeing in her good, high-heeled shoes, as if she were afraid of waking the dead, and touched Isobel's forehead gently.

'Cold,' she said. 'Gone. Hours ago. Poor soul.'

## CHAPTER XI

LIKE MRS GARGRAVE, Holly crossed the room very softly. The room felt haunted by Judy. Her presence there seemed almost as positive as Isobel's.

Mrs Gargrave had withdrawn a step or two from the sofa, then, as if her knees had just given way under her, she sat down suddenly in a chair and began to cry. She cried quietly. The tears simply spilled out of her eyes and ran down her cheeks without her sobbing or making any effort to check them. They could hardly be tears of grief, Holly thought. Mrs Gargrave had never been close to Isobel in any way, ever worked for her or known her well. They were tears provoked simply by the thought of death itself, of how it came to all and would one day come to her too.

Holly picked up the sheet of paper that lay on the floor by the sofa. The paper had Judy's address printed at the top of it. Isobel must have taken it from the desk in Judy's study. Holly recognized the writing as Isobel's. She had used a ball-point pen, no doubt the one that lay on the floor where it had fallen when it had dropped out of her fingers. For the letter had no ending, and the handwriting, which at the beginning was Isobel's normal small, clear, spiky script, collapsed into an almost indecipherable scribble, sloping steeply down the page and stopping in the middle of a sentence.

There was an empty envelope to match the paper on the table. Nothing had been written on the envelope.

There was no address on the letter either. Whether, if she had ever finished it, Isobel would have written Ben's name on the envelope, or 'To the Police,' or what, there was no guessing. The letter, if it could be called a letter, and not simply a statement, began abruptly.

'I am to blame for everything. It is all my fault. I did not mean it to happen, but I should have known that it would. There is no excuse for me. I think I have been slightly insane ever since that girl Loraine came to me with the notes that she had stolen from Lisa Chard, and now that I am sane again and understand what I have done I cannot live with the knowledge. Of course I should not have taken any notice of the girl. Naturally I pretended not to, and spoke to her very sharply for retailing malicious gossip, for which she has done her best to revenge herself on me through Marcus, but the truth was that what she told me drove me out of my mind and made me do what it makes me sick to think of now. What did it really matter if my husband was briefly unfaithful to me? You would never have left me, Ben.'

The writing here was just beginning to straggle wildly.

'You needed me too much. You needed me as much as life itself, because your work is your life and you could not go on with your work without my money. And I have always believed in freedom and that everyone should be able to express his personality and that jealousy is evil. But when it came to the point I couldn't stand it. I thought you should suffer. Not too much, just a little, to punish you for making me suffer, when I thought we were all such a united, happy family. Will my death make you suffer, or have you been hoping for it, because now you can do what you like with my money? Do not let anyone say you are to blame for my death. I have taken all the sleeping-pills I had and drunk some whisky, and thank God, it is beginning to work. No one is to blame except me for everything and I hope that . . .'

What Isobel hoped was just a long zig-zag stroke across the page as the writing became completely out of control.

Holly put the sheet of paper down on the table. Becoming aware of the oozing of blood from her wrist, she tied her handkerchief round it. She thought that the letter had not been begun as one to Ben, but had more probably been meant for the police, but that as the clouds had closed in on Isobel, she had found herself speaking to her husband.

'What does it say?' Mrs Gargrave asked.

Holly gestured at it for Mrs Gargrave to read for herself if she wanted to.

'I haven't got my glasses,' she said.

'It says she did it herself, that no one else is to blame,' Holly said. 'I'd better call the police.'

She went to the study, picked up the telephone and dialled.

She was half-way through dialling when she realized that her fingers, instinctively, had been dialling the Meridens' number, and not that of the police. She hesitated only for an instant, then went on. When the telephone had rung a few times, she heard Marcus's voice answer. He recognized hers as soon as she had said a couple of words and broke in.

'Where are you, Holly? Are you still at Lisa's? Listen, an awful thing's happened. Isobel's disappeared. Ben's telephoned the police, but they haven't got here yet. And I've a horrible feeling it's all my fault, because she believes I killed Judy, and it's driven her out of her mind. She always believed I beat up that old man in the Sea Cave, you know, though I didn't, and now she thinks I killed Judy. But I didn't, I didn't! Even the police don't really think I did. They'd never have let me come home if they did, would they? Do you think they would have, Holly? They can't really think that about me, or they wouldn't have let me come home, would they?'

'Marcus, please, just a minute,' Holly said. 'Can I speak to Andrew?'

'Andrew? Yes, all right. But what do you think—do the police still believe I killed Judy? Did they only let me come home because they haven't enough evidence against me yet? Even if they don't arrest me, are people always going to think I did it?'

'Please, Marcus, just get Andrew, will you?' she said.

'Yes, of course. But what do *you* believe, Holly? You know, Judy and I never had any quarrel. Honestly we didn't. I never threw thc furniture about and attacked her. Yet Isobel's sure I did. I realized it yesterday afternoon after that policeman left. Isobel was so queer. She kept looking at me as if she'd never seen me before. She said it was awful how I told lies, and that what I'd said about burning that paper bag was the last straw. She said some things too about being to blame for everything—'

'Marcus, get me Andrew!' Holly's voice was beginning to rise. 'It's urgent. I've got to speak to him immediately.'

'All right, I'll get him. Hold on.'

There was silence from the other end of the telephone, except for the odd, faint thumping and pinging noises that a telephone makes when it is left off the hook, as if the instrument had a life of its own. Then came the muted sound of footsteps approaching, and Andrew's voice, saying, 'Yes, Holly?'

'Andrew, she's here,' she said. 'Isobel. At Cross Cottage. She's—I'm afraid she's killed herself, Andrew.'

She heard him breathing into the telephone.

She went on hurriedly, 'She brought her sleeping pills with her and took them all, and she's left a—a sort of a letter, which is a sort of a confession, only it isn't exactly, it's—well, it could mean a lot of different things. Will you come here as quickly as you can, Andrew? I haven't telephoned the police yet.'

'I'll come,' he said, 'at once. Are you alone, Holly, or is Lisa with you?'

'Not Lisa,' she said. 'Mrs Gargrave.'

'Well, I'll be there in a few minutes.'

He rang off.

Holly returned to the sitting-room. Mrs Gargrave had not moved from the chair where she was sitting and the tears were still trickling gently down her kindly, rosy face.

'Miss Holly, I haven't told you what I come to see you about,' she said. 'The thing I couldn't get off my mind all last night, so I didn't hardly sleep. I tossed and I turned, and I lay on one side and then on the other, and I couldn't stop thinking. I'm worn out this morning.'

'Well, what did you want to tell me?' Holly asked.

'It's about Loraine.'

'I thought it might be.'

'Miss Holly, Loraine's a good girl, I'd never say anything against her. She's a clever girl too. But there are things she doesn't understand.'

'That I can imagine.'

'Well, there are things you don't understand either, I shouldn't wonder,' Mrs Gargrave said with grave reproof. 'How a girl like Loraine's got to look out for herself, because no one's going to do it for her. I do my best, but who am I? What can I do? I'm just an ignorant woman who's hardly ever been out of Roydon Saint Agnes. I don't hardly go to Helsington more than three or four times a year, and I've never been to London. Think of that, Miss Holly. I've never been to London in my life.'

It seemed to Holly for a moment as if Mrs Gargrave were somehow trying to relate the fact that she had never been to London in her life to Judy's murder and to Isobel's suicide. But of course what Mrs Gargrave was actually trying to do was to express something of a kind that she had never had to before, and she did not know where to begin, how much to say, or what to leave out. So she was approaching her subject obliquely, making little darts into the open then dashing for cover. Her mild complaint against life because she had never been to London was cover, and there was nothing for Holly to do but wait until she chose to emerge again.

She said neutrally, 'A lot of people think London's over-rated.'

'I'd like to see the Christmas decorations in Regent Street,' Mrs Gargrave said.

Holly nodded, as if there were nothing that she wanted more out of life herself. Walking to the window, she stood looking out at the garden, at the apple tree where she had seen Judy picking apples only two days ago, at the borders with dahlias and chrysanthemums in them. By doing that she did not have to go on looking at Isobel.

'But what I want most,' Mrs Gargrave went on, 'is for Loraine to have everything. At my age it doesn't matter much what you see and what you don't, but there's nothing that girl need do without if she's given a chance. So that's why I agreed when she said to me some weeks back, "Don't say a word about me being out yesterday evening," she said. "Whoever asks you, just say I was home all evening." So that's what I done, though I said, "But you don't want Mr Marcus to get into trouble do you? He's your friend," I said. "Him!" she said. "He won't get into any trouble. People like him don't. His mother'll pay his fine for him and that'll be the last anyone'll hear of it. There's other people maybe going to get into trouble," she said, "but not him, you needn't worry." And so I thought, well, I thought, she means the chaps who really beat up that poor old man in the Sea Cave, and as long as they get their due and Loraine keeps out of trouble herself, that's all that matters. I didn't want her to have to go into court. I told you why. Mud sticks. I know all about that. But now all this other trouble's happened, this bad trouble, and I got to thinking . . .'

Mrs Gargrave paused for so long that Holly looked round at her. Mrs Gargrave had stopped crying and was staring straight before her, looking as if she were trying hard to read some writing on the wall, which it was impossible for her to do without her glasses.

At last she said, 'I don't know what I thought except

that I had to tell someone the truth about that evening. And I'd sooner it was you than anyone else. Loraine went to the theatre, the same as usual, that night, then she and Mr Marcus went to the Sea Cave to dance, but they only stayed a little while because they saw some chaps were going to play pop and they didn't want to be mixed up in it, and then they went for a short drive and then Mr Marcus brought Loraine home, and that's all that happened. And that's what Loraine told me that evening, and never said I wasn't to say anything about it till next day, when I know she met Mrs Meriden and had a talk with her, and Mrs Meriden must've said something to hurt Loraine's feelings, because after that she said to me, "Whoever asks you, just say I was home all evening. Don't worry," she said, "he won't get into any trouble. There's other people maybe going to get into trouble, but not him." And so, as I didn't want to say anything myself, I said, "You can count on me, I can keep my mouth shut when I want to." Only now—now—it seems kind of different.'

'There are supposed to be people who saw Marcus in the Sea Cave that evening,' Holly said. 'What about them?'

'Oh, that was just that Fred. The barman. Of course, other people saw Mr Marcus there, but that was earlier. The only one who said he was sure he seen Mr Marcus kicking the old porter was Fred, and he's had it in for Mr Marcus ever since he went wild, getting drunk for the first time in his life, and smashed the place up. Which was not excusable, I wouldn't like you to think I thought that, but no one was hurt and Mr Marcus admitted everything he done and his parents paid the fine and that was the end of that. So I can't see Fred had any call to take revenge, like he did. Revenge, that's what it was, saying he saw Mr Marcus in the fight.'

The doorknocker sounded loudly.

Mrs Gargrave gave a little scream, clapped a hand to her mouth and her tears started to flow again.

'That'll be Mr Meriden,' she said, 'or Mr Andrew. Oh,

those poor children. I've known them all their lives. They were always so happy and so friendly. It doesn't seem right this should've happened to them. What have they ever done to deserve it?'

Her voice followed Holly as she went to the front door.

It was not any of the Meridens who stood there, but Mr Ditteridge.

He came in, bumping his head against the low beam in the ceiling and muttering sourly, 'I shouldn't have done that a second time.' He rubbed the spot that he had bruised and looked at Holly with his air of detached interest. 'Miss Chard told me you might be here,' he said. 'She said you spent the night with her. Odd, it struck me. I got the impression, when I was at the Meridens yesterday, that you were staying with them. Did you have a quarrel with them?'

'Then you don't know . . .'

'Why you moved out? No. But I had a feeling you weren't happy about some of the answers they gave to my questions, and if we could discuss that . . .'

'I mean, you don't know about Mrs Meriden,' Holly said. 'They haven't told you.'

'They've told me she's gone missing,' he said. 'There are men working on that now.'

'I mean, that she's here.'

For the first time since she had met him, he looked startled. 'She spent the night here?'

'She's dead,' Holly said flatly. 'She killed herself.'

For an instant his gaze was neither chilly nor detached, but humanly bewildered and distressed. He gave the bruise on his forehead a sharp blow with his fist, as if he wanted to punish himself.

'Fool!' he said. 'Why didn't I think of that? I thought she'd gone away to save her life, not to take it. Let me see her.'

Holly, who had been standing in the sitting-room doorway, moved to one side and he went in.

He went straight to the sofa on which Isobel lay, bent

over her, took her by the wrist and tried to lift the arm which hung down from her side with the hand trailing on the floor. Its stiffness resisted him. He straightened up, expressionless again.

'I should have thought of it,' he said. 'Where else could she have gone if she hadn't taken her handbag or any money with her and no clothes but what she had on? But I wasn't told anything about her having taken any pills with her.'

'I don't think it was noticed,' Holly said.

'It was too late, anyway, by the time I heard she was missing. I ought to have acted last night. I ought to have taken her away then.'

'Arrested her, do you mean?' Holly exclaimed. 'Do you mean you think she killed my aunt? You can't think that!'

He sighed. 'I do and I don't.' He was looking round the room. 'Didn't she leave a letter?'

Holly pointed. 'Here!'

He picked it up and read it through.

While he was reading, Mrs Gargrave broke in, 'I'm so glad you're here, Mr Ditteridge, because now I can tell you the truth about that Sea Cave business. I just told Miss Holly, but I know I'll have to tell the police—'

He checked her with an irritated frown and read the letter again.

'You've noticed it isn't a confession to the murder,' he said. 'It says that she's to blame for what happened, but not that she picked up that bronze vase and hit Miss Dunthorne over the head with it.'

'No,' Holly said.

'It doesn't even say she was here that evening.'

'No.'

'She couldn't bring herself to say it. She wanted to take the blame—or she almost did, because she'd always done everything she could to look after her family—but she couldn't bring herself to say that.'

'Then who was she trying to protect—or half-trying?'

'You mean you don't know?'

She shook her head.

He sighed, laying the letter down again on the table. 'I thought anyone would guess that when that boy lied about the paper bag. He did lie, you know. Anyone could see that. I saw it myself in his mother's face. Mrs Meriden knew it was a lie, a pointless one, because she knew what had really happened to the bag.'

'What had happened to it?'

'She'd destroyed it herself.'

'But I don't understand . . .' Holly was interrupted once more by the doorknocker.

This time it was Andrew, Kate and Marcus.

Leading them into the sitting-room, Holly saw that Mrs Gargrave had gone. She looked questioningly at Mr Ditteridge.

He said in a low voice, 'I sent her home. She was no use to us here.'

'But some of the things she told me—'

'I can get them later. Anyway, I think I got most of them last night from Mr Floyd. And they're in this letter of Mrs Meriden's.' He turned to Andrew. 'Where's your father? Why hasn't he come with you?'

Andrew made a helpless gesture with both hands, as if he had tried to use them to some purpose, but had failed. Kate had gone to the chair where Mrs Gargrave had been sitting and had collapsed into it, covering her face with her hands. Marcus had gone to his mother and was on his knees beside her, crying like a child.

'I told Ben what Holly said when she telephoned,' Andrew said. 'He acted as if he hadn't heard me. He simply walked off to the workshop. I followed him. He'd locked the door. He didn't usually do that. He shouted at me to go away. I told him all over again what Holly had said. He didn't answer. Then I heard violent noises inside—hammer blows—and something splintering to bits—and curses. And so I thought—I thought the best thing to do was to leave him and bring the other two and come here without him.'

As Andrew finished, he and Mr Ditteridge looked steadily at one another. Andrew was very pale and his features had tightened in the way that made them so remarkably like his mother's, except for the directness of his gaze. The superintendent did not succeed in out-staring him.

'Of course you know what he probably went to the workshop to do,' Mr Ditteridge said quietly.

'I don't know anything,' Andrew answered.

Mr Ditteridge muttered something explosively under his breath and strode out of the room. They heard him talking into the telephone in the study, ordering men to the Meridens' house.

While he was gone, Marcus said sobbingly, 'It was all my fault, wasn't it? She couldn't stand the thought of what I'd done. I told her and I told her I hadn't done it, but somehow I couldn't manage to make her understand.'

Andrew went to him and put a hand on his brother's shoulder.

'You had nothing to do with it, Marcus. You've nothing to blame yourself for. You're just another victim of what's happened.'

'It's that woman,' Kate said savagely. 'Lisa Chard. It's all her fault. There was nothing wrong until she came here.'

'I doubt if that's true,' Andrew said. 'It was all going to happen some time.'

'And she'll never have to pay for it,' Kate said.

'Perhaps that isn't true either,' Andrew answered.

Holly had a feeling that the three of them were talking with a closeness and understanding of one another that excluded her.

'But do you *know* what happened?' she asked. 'Do you know who murdered Judy?'

'Yes, of course,' Andrew said. 'Ben did.'

'How long have you known that?' She felt bitterly angry because he had kept his knowledge to himself.

'Only from the time he locked himself into the workshop. I guessed it almost as soon as it happened, I think, but it was only then I knew.'

'But why did he do it?'

Andrew looked round as Mr Ditteridge came into the room again.

'I think I'll let Mr Ditteridge explain,' he said. 'I expect he knows much more about it all than I do.'

'Somehow I doubt that,' Mr Ditteridge said, 'but I won't argue the point.'

'And how did it happen?' Holly demanded. 'How did Ben and Judy manage to sit drinking in the garden and have a fight there and overturn the furniture after it had got dark and started to rain?'

'Oh, they didn't,' Andrew said. 'I think Mr Ditteridge only encouraged us to think that while he was ferreting around after motives and clues. Are you going to tell Miss Dunthorne all about it, Mr Ditteridge?'

Mr Ditteridge looked round the room at Kate, sitting with her face still covered, at Marcus, kneeling by his mother's body, at Andrew, standing over Marcus, and Holly, stiff and still in the middle of the room.

'Very well,' Mr Ditteridge said, 'but I suggest we go into the garden until my men arrive. And I'll tell you what I surmise. Remember, it hasn't been proved. And as it doesn't look as if there'll ever be a trial, I dare say it never will be. It's what I shall have to put forward at the inquest, however. I'm sorry—I'd be glad for all your sakes if it didn't have to be done, but some things can't be helped.'

He led the way out into the garden.

Kate dropped on to one of the garden chairs. Feeling the chill of the puddle on it, she leapt to her feet again, swearing hysterically. Andrew tilted the chair to get rid of the puddle, then mopped the seat with his handkerchief.

'It's all right now, sit down,' he said, pressing Kate back on to the chair. He treated another chair in the same way for Holly, while Marcus flopped down on the damp flagstones of the terrace, drawing his knees up to his chin and wrapping his long arms round his legs. Andrew himself remained standing, grasping the back of one of the chairs with both hands and leaning on it.

Mr Ditteridge withdrew a little way from them all, standing looking at them with a frown, as if they were an audience who he feared might prove troublesome and heckle him. He started to speak, then cut off the words with a sharp closing of his jaws, appeared to think deeply, then started again.

'I'm not sure I ought to say any of this,' he said, 'and you needn't believe any of it if you can find a better explanation to fit the facts. But the way I think things happened is this. It all began when Miss Chard came to live here and started an affair with Mr Meriden. It isn't my job to say who seduced whom—it happened, that's all I can say, as I got out of Mr Floyd yesterday evening. He's been having an affair with Miss Chard himself, and he's jealous and observant. And we'll get all the corroboration we want, if it's needed, from Loraine Gargrave, who was doing domestic work for Miss Chard when the affair with Mr Meriden was at its height. Loraine had got herself the job because she thought Miss Chard might be useful to her in the career she'd chosen, as she was. She got Loraine in with the Market Theatre people. But then Loraine thought she could get more out of Miss Chard than that, and Miss Chard only laughed at her. And Loraine's a young woman who won't stand being laughed at, so she took her revenge on Miss Chard by going to Mrs Meriden—that's all in her letter—and telling her all about her husband's love affair. And Mrs Meriden only spoke to her sharply for spreading malicious gossip, so that's why Loraine took the line she did about the Sea Cave affair. All clear so far?'

No one answered. No one was even looking at him except Andrew, for Kate had covered her face with her hands again, and Marcus had hidden his on his knees, and

Holly was watching Andrew, wanting with desperation to offer comfort, but knowing that any of the easy kinds were not for now.

Mr Ditteridge went on, 'What Loraine didn't know, of course, was what the effect of what she'd said had really been on Mrs Meriden. If she'd guessed what it was going to be, I think even that girl might've hesitated about doing what she did. Quite simply, Mrs Meriden decided she wasn't going to say anything to her husband about his affair with Miss Chard, but all the same she was going to punish him for it. So she wrote him a blackmailing letter—'

'*She* wrote to him?' Andrew interrupted.

'Yes, she wrote an anonymous letter to him, telling him that unless he paid five hundred pounds, according to certain instructions she gave him, the writer would tell her, Mrs Meriden, about his affair with Miss Chard.'

'But she—she herself—gave him the five hundred pounds!' Andrew exclaimed. 'You found that out and she admitted it.'

'Yes, it's an unusual situation,' Mr Ditteridge said. 'Your mother blackmailed your father with the threat that she would reveal his love affair to herself, then gave him the money to pay the blackmail with.'

As they were all silent, he tugged at his long chin. He went on, 'Can't say I've ever heard of another case just like it in all my experience. I don't even know just what crime she committed, if it was one at all. You couldn't exactly call it demanding money with menaces, and though I've been speaking of blackmail, I don't think you could really have made it stick. If she could just have managed to go on living with herself, I don't believe anybody could have touched her. Of course, you must understand that the money in itself was totally unimportant. Perhaps that's why the sum wasn't larger. She wanted to punish him, that was all, to make him suffer, as she was suffering. And as he was entirely dependent on her, not just for ordinary support, but to keep that work of his going, that work that meant such a lot to him, he must have been very frightened, he must have suffered a good deal, don't you think?'

Kate gave an abrupt shiver, dropped her hands from her face, looked up at Mr Ditteridge and said, 'I can see her doing it, you know. She never came out in the open and said anything against you, but she'd get at you all the same.'

'Shut up!' Marcus growled with his face still hidden. 'Shut up!'

Kate kept a wide-eyed stare on Mr Ditteridge's face. 'Go on,' she said.

He resumed, 'I don't know how he got the money from her, what it was he said he needed it for.'

'I know,' Holly said. 'I heard them talking about it yesterday morning. New tools, they said.'

'Thank you. Well, then he followed the instructions the blackmail note had given him. He went to Cleeve and Coleford and bought some handkerchiefs, which they put in one of their striped red and green paper bags, and he put the money that he'd just got from Mrs Meriden in the bag and took it to the Crown and put it on the shelf of that so-called Ladies' Cloakroom in the passage. Anyone passing had only to reach out and take it, which was a risk for Mrs Meriden, but one she decided to take because it was an easy place both for him to leave it and for her to pick it up from inconspicuously. But then Mr Meriden did something he hadn't been instructed to do. He went and had lunch in the Snack Bar at the Crown, where he could watch the comings and goings from the passage where the Ladies' Cloakroom is. And what did he see? He saw his wife and Miss Dunthorne come in and have a drink in the bar together, then go to the restaurant, and later on come out together. Then all of a sudden Miss Dunthorne came back, collected the paper bag with the money in it, and went out again. So wasn't it natural for him to assume that Miss Dunthorne was the blackmailer?'

'I'm sorry, Holly,' Andrew said, 'I've got to say it—suppose she was.'

Mr Ditteridge shook his head. 'There was no five hundred pounds in the coffee canister in Cross Cottage on the night of her murder. I looked there myself. She didn't take it home with her that day. The money was put there later by Mrs Meriden, who didn't want us, or her husband to find it in her possession. So she slipped out of the house—everyone was used to her wandering about in the night—and brought it here. But there was no paper bag from Cleeve and Coleford in the cottage. What happened at the Crown, I believe, is this. Mrs Meriden, knowing that her husband could see who removed the bag from the shelf in the passage, left it there, and only when she and Miss Dunthorne were outside, pretended to remember that she'd left a parcel behind, and asked Miss Dunthorne to go back and fetch it for her, while she was getting the car out of the car-park. We know that Miss Dunthorne did go back into the hotel, went to the Ladies' Cloakroom and left again, carrying that paper bag. And Mr Meriden certainly saw her. And later that day, because of it, he murdered her. He was a very, very frightened man, very frightened of what it would mean to him if his wife divorced him.'

'But if he'd come here and accused Miss Dunthorne of blackmailing him,' Andrew said, 'wouldn't she have told him the truth?'

'And would he have believed her? With his own eyes he'd seen her take the money. The only alternative, that his wife was the blackmailer, hadn't entered his head yet. It was only yesterday that he understood that, when your brother Marcus said he'd actually seen the paper bag from Cleeve and Coleford in the house and had burnt it himself.'

'But that was a lie!' Marcus cried. 'I never saw it. I never burnt it.'

Mr Ditteridge looked at him with a mild degree of pity in his eyes. 'And your mother started so violently that no one could have failed to see it, certainly not your father, who was watching her like a hawk, wondering how much she'd guessed about him. I'm afraid that lie of yours was one of the kind that only reveals the truth.'

Marcus lifted his head. 'You're all wrong,' he said. 'You're wrong from beginning to end. I killed Judy. I came here, and we had a drink together, and we talked about Loraine, and—and somehow I got annoyed with her, and then—then I had a sort of black-out, and the next thing I knew, I was standing over her and she was dead. My father had nothing to do with it.'

Mr Ditteridge shook his head. 'A good try, boy, but it won't do. He killed her. He came here just about when it was getting dark. It must have been only a few minutes after you'd left. He came in by the french window. I suppose the light was on, but she hadn't drawn the curtains yet. They had their quarrel, he killed her and he began a search for the money. But then he'd have realised that the light in the room could be seen from the road and that anyone, looking in, could see him, and also that Miss Holly Dunthorne was to be expected back at any minute. So he turned out the light and left in a hurry, and going out like that suddenly into the rain and darkness, he wouldn't have been able to see anything for a moment, and this green these chairs are painted wouldn't have shown up in the darkness anyhow, so he fell over them, upsetting them all, and later that gave him a sort of alibi . . .'

He stopped as footsteps sounded on the path round the cottage.

A young constable appeared. He stood still when he saw the group on the terrace, then came to attention, carefully avoiding looking at anyone but Mr Ditteridge. His fresh young face was mottled with shock.

'We found him, sir,' he said. 'Had to break the door down and there he was, stabbed himself in the chest with a knife he had there. Terrible force behind the blow. Those great hands of his . . .' The young man gagged slightly. He had not yet seen much violent death. 'But first—first he must have taken a mallet and smashed a little table there to smithereens. Queer thing . . . I mean, to do a thing like that when you're going to kill yourself. Pretty thing it must have been too. But it's smashed past mending.'

Mr Ditteridge looked at Andrew. 'You knew he was going to do this.'

'I told you,' Andrew said, 'I didn't know anything.'

'You guessed his intention.'

'What's a guess? And I'd call it his choice. Hadn't I any right to leave him freedom of choice? He and my mother always left as much as possible to us, so didn't we owe them the same in return? If they chose to destroy each other . . .' Andrew's voice shook suddenly, grew hoarse and stopped. His hand reached out blindly for Holly's.

# CHAPTER XII

> "'*Architect-designed residence on outskirts of picturesque village of Roydon Saint Agnes, five miles from Helsington with good train service to London. Three reception rooms, three bedrooms, two bathrooms, oil-fired central heating, garage, attractive garden. Offers around £18,000 . . .*'"

KATE LOWERED the copy of *The Sunday Times* that she was reading, and looked over the top of it at Holly.

'That's the Chard woman's house, like to bet?' she said.

'So her love affair with it didn't last long,' Holly replied. 'She once told me she'd given up marriage in favour of love affairs with houses.'

'Pity she didn't stick to them exclusively,' Kate said.

She had been sharing Holly's London flat with her for the last six months, moving in as soon as Holly's parents, who had come home briefly from Australia, had returned to

Sydney. Each girl had a bedroom of her own and they shared the living-room. The arrangement was working fairly well. Holly cleaned the flat and Kate did most of the cooking. She was not an inspired cook, like her mother, but was more competent than Holly had expected.

Kate had not stuck to her plan of going to a Secretarial School. She had somehow got herself a job on a woman's magazine as assistant to the beauty editor, and had discovered, she declared, that she had at last found her vocation. In the evenings, if she was not out with one of the men who were trying to attach themselves to her in ever greater numbers, she either made herself clothes, with remarkable success, or else wrote little love stories which a variety of magazines were buying with increasing enthusiasm. She was revealing herself, in fact, as a talented low-brow, who would undoubtedly end up, Holly thought, as a very rich and successful woman.

Not that Kate needed money. Like Andrew and Marcus, she had inherited more than enough to live on comfortably from her parents. But the discovery that she could compete successfully in the working world excited her and stimulated her.

'You know, the trouble for me at home,' she had said recently to Holly, 'was that the atmosphere was so terribly rarefied. Everyone was supposed to be good at something fearfully significant. So I spent my time feeling I must be some kind of mental deficient. But now, in my way, I'm not doing so badly, am I? I know nothing I do is of the least importance to anybody, still, what I do, I do as well as I can, and that gives me quite a feeling of satisfaction. I'd hate to realize I was beginning to take myself too seriously, but I do love getting my pay-packet, and those little cheques for my stories, and finding I'm not too utterly hopeless at everything. It's different for Andrew and Marcus, of course, who are good at things that matter, but I'm just a happy little hack, and the Lord be praised for it.'

What Marcus was good at that mattered Holly was not sure. At the moment he was filling in time, driving a busload of tourists overland to Bombay. At infrequent intervals he sent picture-postcards of places of interest en route, always promising to write at greater length, which he never did. The news that he managed to cram on to the postcards generally related to the misbehaviour of the bus. He would be driving it home again soon with a fresh load of tourists. Then, in the autumn, he was going to the University of Sussex to study Biology.

It was Andrew who had overcome Marcus's reluctance to going to a university and had succeeded in this only on the understanding that the university should be one of the new ones and as untraditional as possible. Holly felt no certainty that he would end up a biologist. He might have a long way to go before he discovered how to use his great, unwieldy strength. And unless he were exceptionally lucky, other people would always see to it that his path was fraught with difficulties. That vulnerability of his would always invite trouble.

Andrew had returned to Canada. But that had been only for the time being. Before his leave of absence was over, he had been offered and had accepted a job in a big computer firm in Edinburgh, which was setting up a department of Model Simulation, of which he was to be the head, and on the day that Kate noticed the advertisement of Lisa Chard's house, he was flying back to London, and Holly had started to work on her hair and her make-up before setting off to meet him at Heathrow.

She looked very calm as she went about it. She had recently taken to wearing her hair up, in a way that Kate, an expert now in such things, had shown her, and there was the slightly worrying question on Holly's mind of whether, first, Andrew would notice it at all, and second, would like it if he did. It made her look older, sleeker, more poised. But she did not feel older or sleeker or the least bit more poised when she thought of seeing him again, and felt half-inclined, as she looked at herself in the mirror, to take all the pins out and let her hair flop around her shoulders in its old way.

But that showed a deplorable lack of courage, when you had made up your mind to start a new life anyway. For that had been agreed on in the letters that had passed between London and Canada. Soberly and thoughtfully agreed, because after the sort of events that had shaken them all last year, no one, of course, should do anything impulsively or purely emotionally. So time was to be allowed for Andrew to settle into the new job in Edinburgh, and for Holly to finish working for her Ph.D., and for the two of them to get to know one another again in a normal atmosphere.

Only, as it happened, nothing about the atmosphere today felt normal. It vibrated with impulse and emotion. And that, together with the spring sunshine, lighting up the fresh green of the plane trees in the street, made it seem by far the most extraordinary and wonderful day that had happened since the one on which Holly had returned from Portugal and seen Andrew again, after those four years, and everyone had been happy and cheerful and nobody had been murdered yet . . .

No, what a falsification of the facts that was. Perhaps Holly was the only person who had been happy that day. And Judy too. For all that was to happen had already been set in motion. Loraine Gargrave had been at her death-dealing work. As, no doubt, she still was, and would continue to be for the rest of a long and successful life, knifing anyone who happened to get in her way, or to offend her, until she reached the top. She was on the way up already. Kate and Holly had seen her on television only a few nights before. She had had a very small part, but there was no doubt about it, the dreadful girl had stood out, she had talent, she would, as Lisa Chard had recognized, arrive sooner or later.

What had happened to Lisa, or where she was, Holly did

not know. The play, *Designs on Life*, was still running in London. Stephen Floyd, she had heard, had married. His wife was a girl who had been an actress at the Market Theatre, a girl called Wendy, who, Holly seemed to remember, had wanted cheese for her lunch. And Cross Cottage had been sold, and some of the better furniture from it was here in Holly's flat, for Judy had left her all that she possessed. And Mrs Gargrave, whose old father had died one night in his sleep, was working, when her veins allowed it, for the new couple who had bought the cottage.

The Meriden house still stood empty. There was talk of a major highway being driven through the grounds, close to it, and when the house had been put up for sale, there had been no offers. Kate had picked out certain pieces of her father's furniture and brought them to her room in the flat. The rest had been put into store. He had often said of it himself that long after he was dead, each piece would become a collector's item and that the prices that they would fetch would fill the public with awe. Perhaps he was right. And if that day ever came, would anyone ever worry about his personal history? Would anyone shudder, even briefly, at eating dinner, cheerfully, with friends, off a table that had been made by the hands of a murderer . . .?

Sometimes Holly thought of him as he had been in the evening after he had killed Judy. He had sat still in the car and cried. He had told Holly it was because he had once been in love with Judy. But hadn't it really been for himself, because he had already foreseen the consequences of his action, had known that the only sort of life that mattered to him was at an end, that there would be no more designing, no more loving craftsmanship?

'Oh God, I'm going to be late, I'm going to be late!' Holly exclaimed suddenly, leaping up from the stool at her dressing-table. 'I simply haven't been watching the time.'

'Darling, you've never had your eye off the clock for the

last hour,' Kate replied. 'And I meant to tell you, I'm going to the zoo with Terry this afternoon. Why the zoo I couldn't tell you, except that Terry has a sort of thing about zoos. He's been wanting to take me there ever since we met. So I said all right, let's go tomorrow. And so, if Andrew should want a quiet rest after his flight, you see, the flat'll be empty. Now run along, or you won't have nearly long enough to wait at Heathrow. It's a wonderful thing, waiting, isn't it, it's a sort of delicious agony, when you know it's only going to be for a very little while longer?'

# Ngaio Marsh

'The finest writer in the English language of the pure, classical, puzzle whodunit. Among the Crime Queens, Ngaio Marsh stands out as an Empress.' *Sun*. 'Her work is as near flawless as makes no odds: character, plot, wit, good writing and sound technique.' *Sunday Times*. 'The brilliant Ngaio Marsh ranks with Agatha Christie and Dorothy Sayers.' *Times Literary Supplement*.

**Last Ditch**

**Vintage Murder**

**Death and the Dancing Footman**

**Death at the Dolphin**

**Hand in Glove**

**Colour Scheme**

**Scales of Justice**

**Singing in the Shrouds**

**Spinsters in Jeopardy**

**A Clutch of Constables**

**Death in a White Tie**

**Dead Water**